"Don't you see? There's one donor coming in. Only one. Who will the doctors save? Who will get the transplant?"

For a moment Josh stared blankly as her question sank in. "Katie, you don't know for sure there's only one donor."

"Yes, I do. There's only one. One heart. Two lungs. The doctor said the donor's family had given permission for all her organs to be donated." Katie's voice had risen with the tide of panic rising in her. "There're two people in need and only one heart."

ONE LAST WISH

Lurlene McDaniel

She Died Too Young

BANTAM BOOKS

NEW YORK · TORONTO · LONDON · SYDNEY · AUCKLAND

RL 5, age 10 and up

SHE DIED TOO YOUNG

A Bantam Book / March 1996

One Previous Edition

The Starfire logo is a registered trademark of Bantam Books,
a division of Bantam Doubleday Dell Publishing Group, Inc.
Registered in U.S. Patent and Trademark Office and elsewhere.

ISBN 0-553-57094-3

Published simultaneously in the United States and Canada

Bantam Books are published by Bantam Books, a division of Bantam
Doubleday Dell Publishing Group, Inc. Its trademark, consisting of the
words "Bantam Books" and the portrayal of a rooster, is Registered in
U.S. Patent and Trademark Office and in other countries. Marca Registrada. Bantam Books, 1540 Broadway, New York, New York 10036.

PRINTED IN THE UNITED STATES OF AMERICA

RAD   0 9 8 7 6 5 4 3 2 1

*I would like to express my gratitude to
Tennessee Donor Services,
whose valuable input helped
in the creation of this manuscript*

and

*To B.C.H.
Thank you for the beautiful music.*

One

Katie O'Roark watched her boyfriend, Josh Martel, read through her friend Chelsea James's letter. They were sitting in a wicker swing on her front porch in the warm September afternoon.

Katie reread the letter over Josh's shoulder:

Dear Katie,

I'm writing to you from the hospital. The first thing my doctor did when I got home from Jenny House last week was admit me. Some homecoming. Of course, it wasn't a big surprise. I told you just before we left it was what I thought he'd do. But it sure isn't any fun.

They're running all sorts of tests (again!), but I know the results already: My poor old heart is plain old tired. I've tried telling it that we're both only fifteen and it has no right to poop out on me, but it's not listening. I'm on oxygen, and until yesterday I was spiking a fever. They've got the fever under control now, thank you very much. My parents are worried and trying to act brave, but they're driving me crazy.

It's looking more and more like I'll be a candidate for a heart transplant. Of course, I'm scared, but after having met you this summer, I know that a new heart is my only hope for a normal life. Just look at you. New heart. New life. Who knows, maybe I'll even give you some competition on the track once I get the transplant. (Just kidding—I've never run a single day in my life thanks to my bum heart. Why start now?)

If there's a bright spot in this whole thing—See how I learned to think positively over the summer? You and Amanda taught me positive thinking—it's that I'll be coming to Ann Arbor once I go on the beeper for a transplant. Which puts me in the same city as you. I can't tell you how much that gives me courage. Knowing that I won't have to go through this thing alone.

So just as soon as I know what's going on, I'll contact you. Hope you got started back in school without any problems. Lucky you! A senior and all. I may not ever get to run a foot race, but maybe at long last, I'll get to attend a real school and have a real life. Bye for now. Say hi to Josh for me.

I've written this news to Lacey too, but who knows how she'll take it? You know Lacey—she's

not keen on sick people even though her diabetes
makes her one of us.

Love and stuff,
Chelsea

As he handed the letter back to Katie, she said, "I know exactly what she's going through. I'm writing her today. As soon as she comes to Ann Arbor, I'll be by her side every minute."

"Well, don't forget, you've got a life too," Josh said.

His words stung Katie. "What's that supposed to mean? I'm surprised you'd say such a thing. She's my friend. I can't abandon her."

"I'm not asking you to. But, Katie, it's been a long summer with you away. Now that school's started, I want things back to normal for us. Dates. Fun."

Although she thought Josh was acting selfish, she didn't want to have an argument with him. "Don't worry, we'll get back to normal," she answered. "But you know how important Chelsea is to me. I don't think I could stand it if she . . ." Katie didn't finish her sentence, as tears pooled in her eyes.

Josh put his arm around her and pulled her against his chest. "Chelsea won't be like Amanda," he said. "She's going to come through this with flying colors. You'll see."

"I guess I'm not over Amanda," she admitted. "I thought that coming home and starting school would make the hurt go away, but it hasn't."

"I know. You stuff it down inside, but then when you least expect it, it sneaks out and smacks you square in the face."

Of course, Josh knows, Katie thought. His brother, Aaron, had died right in front of his eyes only two years before.

Josh lifted her chin and gazed at her face. "I miss Aaron every day, and on days when I'm having too much fun, I start to feel guilty because he's not alive to have fun too. I have to really watch that I don't get morbid. Knowing his heart's inside you helps." Josh hugged her hard. "You'll always miss Amanda, but you can't let it take over your life."

She knew what he said was true. "I wonder what it would be like to be like the other kids at our high school—the ones who don't have to worry about dying, or watching their friends die."

"You mean worry about grades or who's going to win the football game?" The corners of his eyes crinkled as he teased.

"Or who's going to ask whom to the homecoming dance," Katie joked.

"No worry there. You've already got a date," he said, and kissed the tip of her nose. "As I see it, Katie, my love, you only have to figure out where you're going to college. Any progress?"

Another touchy subject, she thought. Just that morning she'd had a confrontation with her parents about it. They wanted her to attend the University of Michigan and live at home next year. But she wanted a track scholarship, and that could mean going to a college far away. "No. I'm sending off a letter to that track coach I met at the Transplant Games two summers ago. You remember him? His son had had a kidney transplant."

"I remember him. Arizona, wasn't it?" Josh looked glum. "You know how I feel about it. I want you nearby. I mean, there's no way I can go away to college—too expensive, and my grades aren't exactly merit scholarship material. I have to stay here for college, live with Gramps, and work. There's no other way."

Katie felt the now familiar twinge of guilt. Going away to college meant leaving Josh, her family, and her medical support staff. But her cardiologist had told her that her transplanted heart was in fine shape, and as long as she took her antirejection medications and took care of herself, she could continue doing well. "No one's offered me a scholarship, so I may have to stay put."

"You could go if you want to," Josh said. "You still have some of your One Last Wish money."

That was true. A portion of the one hundred thousand dollars was socked away in the bank. Now that Katie knew the identity of her benefactor, a girl named Jennifer Warren Crawford, who'd died in 1978 after setting up the One Last Wish Foundation, the origin of the money she'd been given was no longer a mystery. "That money may have to go toward keeping me in my medications," she told Josh. "Dad's medical benefits from his health insurance have a cap and will run out someday. Then I'll have to pay for my medications some other way."

"You'll earn a fortune being the top female runner in the country."

"Is that why you love me? Because of my money?" she teased, hoping to distract him from questioning her about college. She didn't know what she was going to do, and she was weary of thinking about it. Right now, she had Chelsea and her medical problems on the brain. Plus starting school. And the loss of Amanda.

Josh grinned. "That's what turns me on about you all right. All that money."

He snuggled against her neck, and goose bumps skidded up her spine. "The neighbors might be watching," she said.

"Let them watch," Josh replied, and kissed her softly on the mouth.

Katie was doing homework when Chelsea called three days later. "It's official," Chelsea said. "I'm going on the beeper."

Katie felt her stomach lurch. With the phone receiver clamped to her ear, she sprawled across her bed. "When are you coming?"

"Mom's making a mountain of arrangements now. She's coming with me while Dad holds down the fort. He'll visit every weekend he can, but somebody's got to stay and work and pay the bills."

Katie heard the anxiety in her friend's voice. "I'll be here for you. And so will Josh."

"That's the only good part of this whole thing. The worst is not knowing how long I'll have to wait for my transplant. My doctor says the average wait is close to six months for a heart."

The information surprised Katie. She'd been much luckier—if she could think of Aaron's death as a piece of luck. Her wait hadn't been long at all. She forced her thoughts away from that course. Nothing could bring Aaron back, and she was grateful to be alive. "Maybe you won't have to wait that long," she offered hopefully.

"Who knows? Mom's calling realtors in your area and trying to find us an apartment close to the hospital. She says we'd better plan on the long haul instead of trying to rent a motel room and live like gypsies. I think it's better too. This way, I'll be able to bring some of my things with me and make the place more like a home instead of a waiting cell."

Katie thought the prospects of being cooped up in a rented apartment and not knowing anybody dismal also. All at once, an idea occurred to her. "Maybe that won't be necessary," she said, sitting upright on her bed.

"What do you mean?"

Katie's voice grew with excitement. "We have a big house, and my parents know just what your mother's going through. And you and I are best friends. Chelsea, what would you think about living here with us until your beeper goes off?"

Two

"SO WHEN'S CHELSEA moving in?" Josh asked Katie as they threaded their way along the crowded hallway heading for morning classes.

"This weekend. My parents were absolute angels about it. They've been on the phone with Chelsea's folks every day ironing out details. Chelsea's getting the guest room next to mine, and her mom, Lorraine, will be moving into my mom's sewing room. Mom's cleaning it up to make it more comfortable."

"Your parents are pretty great," Josh said.

Katie knew how fond Josh was of her folks. Probably because his own parents were such failures. His father, an alcoholic, abused his mother. That's why Josh and Aaron had moved across several states and into their grandfather's home in the first place. Katie said, "Since fall's my dad's busy season at the newspaper, Mom's really looking forward to having the company. And since she understands just what Chelsea's parents are facing—"

The first tardy bell interrupted Katie's sentence. Josh bent forward and brushed her cheek with a kiss. "Oops! I've got to run. If I'm late for class . . ."

"See you after school," Katie called as he sprinted off down the hall. She marched into honors English and took her seat.

"Did you do the assignment?"

Katie turned to the boy sitting behind her who'd asked the question. His name was Garrison Reilly, new to Ann Arbor High and distinctively good-looking. She purposely avoided gazing into his deep brown eyes. "Didn't you?"

"Are you kidding? When my dad's the chairman of the English department at the University of Michigan, what choice do I have?"

His grin was infectious, and Katie returned it in spite of herself. "I figure that puts you at an unfair advantage. What chance do we mere mortals have when you're wired into the mother lode of English proficiency?"

Garrison's grin grew broader. "Take it from me, *you* have more than a chance in my book."

She rolled her eyes good-naturedly. "Isn't that a line in some famous book or other?"

"A line? What an unkind cut! Yours is the first pretty, friendly face I've met in this school."

"Oh, cut it out," Katie said with a laugh, playing

on his words. "We're all friendly here at Ann Arbor High. Didn't you read your orientation packet?"

His eyes glowed with mischief. "I read where there's a football game this Friday night. You going?"

Suddenly, Katie realized they were flirting with each other. *What's wrong with me?* she asked herself. She experienced an overwhelming sense of disloyalty toward Josh.

When she didn't answer his question, Garrison gave her a questioning look. "Was it something I said?"

"What?"

"You checked out on me. What did I say to cause a retreat? Football games shouldn't be that bad a topic for conversation."

"Nothing. I, uh, just"—she glanced up—"see our teacher," she finished lamely. "Class is starting."

"So can we continue this discussion later? After school, maybe?"

Katie felt her cheeks flame red. She flipped open her book and buried her nose in it. "I have something else to do."

"Well, tomorrow's another day," Garrison said over her shoulder. "Scarlett O'Hara said that in *Gone with the Wind.*" She heard him shift back into his chair.

Katie sat staring at the book without really seeing it. Her heart was thudding and her blood racing as she realized it was more than guilt she was feeling. She was attracted to Garrison Reilly, and understanding that interest washed over her like cold water. Quickly, she scribbled Josh's name three times on the cover of her notebook, as if by doing so, she could make the strange and peculiar sensations she experienced toward Garrison fade away.

Chelsea arrived that weekend, and even though Chelsea's mother hovered at her side, Katie was glad to see that she could navigate the stairs under her own power. When Chelsea was settled in bed and everyone else had gone down to move Mrs. James's belongings into the converted sewing room, Katie exclaimed, "I'm so glad you're here. We're going to have fun while you wait."

Chelsea and her mom had brought a few pieces of furniture from Chelsea's own bedroom in a U-haul trailer. Along with some medical equipment—a portable oxygen tank was propped by the head of the bed—they transformed the guest room. Katie was relieved to see that Chelsea didn't have to be tethered to the tank day and night. At least, not yet.

"You don't know how glad I am to be staying with you instead of in some apartment." Chelsea glanced around the room—at the fresh bouquet of flowers on the dresser, at the TV set, at the pretty lace curtains and glittery "Welcome" banner Katie had stretched across them. "Everything except a virtual reality game."

"Yeah. Well, I didn't want you to get *too* comfortable."

"The only place I'd rather be is Jenny House." Chelsea's voice sounded breathy, and her lips held a bluish cast.

Katie remembered her own pain from her medical ordeal. Still, she smiled brightly and said, "You've got that right. There's no place better than Jenny House. As soon as you're able, I think we should go visit."

"Could we?"

"Look, we don't know how long it'll take for the transplant center to find you a heart, but as long as you're feeling and doing well, you don't have to be confined to bed."

"Tell that to my mother."

"That's what *my* mother is supposed to do— help *yours* not to act too hyper. And believe me, my mom's a pro when it comes to acting hyper. She almost drove me and Dad to the nut house. But after the Transplant Games, once she saw that I wasn't going to shatter, she shaped right up." Katie grinned. "Yours will too."

"You don't know my mother. She's spent my whole lifetime hovering over me and my crummy heart. It's her career!"

Katie laughed. "Once your transplant is complete and you're out of danger, she'll have to find a new career. You're going to feel so good!"

"So, you think the center will allow me to take a trip? What if my beeper goes off while I'm out of town?"

"As long as you feel pretty good and if you only stay away for a couple of days, I'm sure it'll be fine.

And if they find you a donor, we'll fly straight back."

"Dr. Hooper, my doctor at home, told me that I'd have to participate in some kind of therapy group," Chelsea said. "Is that true?"

"It's not so bad. Actually, the shrinks need to check you out to see if you'd make a good organ recipient."

"What do you mean?"

"I'm sure they've told you how few organs there are to go around. Lots of people need them, and not enough people are donating their organs or the organs of people they love who die in some tragedy."

"You mean like Josh's brother?"

"Exactly." Katie remembered the things she'd been told while she awaited her transplant. In some ways, it seemed so long ago. And she'd been so sick. "Anyway, just because someone needs an organ doesn't mean she can emotionally handle getting one. Not everyone can handle being sick or getting well."

Chelsea nodded. "You mean like Lacey and the way she acts as if she doesn't even have a disease."

"Exactly. Unless she accepts her diabetes, she'd be a poor choice for a pancreas transplant, for instance. The doctors have to be sure a recipient will take care of herself, or what's the use of transplanting? I mean, if the doctors give you a new organ and you don't take care of yourself—" Katie shrugged to make her point.

"The transplant would be a waste," Chelsea concluded. "Plus it could have gone to someone else who would have taken better care of herself. Is that what you mean?"

"Exactly." Katie fiddled with the bedcovers while she talked. "Besides, you'll be put in some therapy group with others waiting for transplants. I was too sick to attend one, and my transplant opportunity came up quickly, so I never went to group."

Chelsea made a face. "It doesn't sound like much fun—waiting around with a bunch of people desperate for an organ. In fact, it sounds sort of ghoulish to me. 'Excuse me, miss, did you need a heart or a kidney? Could we pass you a lung?'" Chelsea mimicked.

"I didn't think so either," Katie admitted after laughing over Chelsea's black humor. "But after spending the summer at Jenny House, after meeting so many kids who were sick with something or other, I can see how it does help to meet others like yourself. It makes you feel less alone."

Chelsea closed her eyes, as if gathering her strength to continue talking. "Going to Jenny House and meeting you and Lacey and Amanda was the best thing that ever happened to me." The mention of Amanda caused both Katie and Chelsea to pause. "Will it always hurt this way when we think about her?"

"Josh says no. He lost his brother, and he says you never forget, but you learn to adjust. I trust him because he's been there."

"Will Josh come by to see me today?"

"Tonight."

Chelsea smiled. "Good. Too bad there's only one of him." Her hand slipped into Katie's. "Lucky you."

Katie glanced away. She still was upset and surprised at the way Garrison had made her feel. In class Friday morning, he'd said, "If you change your mind about the football game tonight, I'll be sitting near the fifty-yard line."

She'd shaken her head no. She knew she'd be with Josh. "I'm busy."

"Until next time, then," he'd answered.

She knew there wouldn't be a next time. She now avoided looking at him.

Katie glanced down at Chelsea and saw that her energy was sapped. She tugged the covers up under Chelsea's chin and stood. "I'll let you get some rest."

"When will you come back?" Chelsea sounded as if she was afraid to be alone.

"When you wake up, ring this bell." She handed Chelsea the bell she'd used to summon her mother when she'd been so sick. "And I'll come running."

"You're my best friend, Katie."

"Same here." But when Katie left the room, she leaned against the door frame, suddenly apprehensive. How was she going to juggle Chelsea, Josh, and school—especially when Garrison Reilly made her feel quivery whenever she gazed into his eyes?

Three

❦

ENVIOUS. CHELSEA ADMITTED to herself that envy was the overriding emotion she felt whenever she was with Katie. To Chelsea's way of thinking, Katie had it all. Katie had already been through the heart transplant procedure, and she'd survived it with flying colors. Chelsea knew the statistics by heart: Over eighty percent of all heart recipients were still alive a year following the procedure. And almost seventy percent were living five years after a transplant.

"The odds are in your favor," Katie told her enthusiastically. But knowing such facts didn't make Chelsea's fear go away. If only she could be confident the way Katie was!

Chelsea kept up a brave front, especially in front of her mother. But deep inside, she struggled against the rising tide of doubts. Certainly, the summer at Jenny House had helped her face some of the fears she'd carried with her all her life. She'd done things she'd never even dreamed of doing before. Daring things, like riding horses and playing games and climbing up to the special mountain plateau Amanda had discovered.

But those fears were different from the one that gnawed at her now. Now that she was actually on the beeper, now that she was actually waiting for her own heart to be exchanged for a healthy one, she was scared to death. And Chelsea wouldn't share the fears with anyone. Not her parents. Not Katie. Not even the doctors in charge of the therapy group she was attending at the university's transplant center.

As she waited for the therapy session to begin, Chelsea glanced around the small auditorium at the assortment of kids who, like herself, were awaiting heart or lung transplants. At the first group meeting, Dr. Cummings, the psychiatrist leading the group, had welcomed, "At this center alone, approximately five thousand patients are on the beeper for hearts and lungs, and the smallest segment consists of kids ten to eighteen."

Dr. Cummings had split the group, putting younger kids into one session and older ones into another. They were to meet twice a week to discuss their potential transplants and their feelings. Chelsea walked to a refreshment table and helped herself to some food.

"Don't you think this seems more like a Girl

Scout social than a head-shrink program?" a girl standing beside Chelsea asked in a thick drawl.

Chelsea turned. She saw a girl with frizzy red hair, blue eyes, and a million freckles smiling at her. "Too many boys to be a Girl Scout social," Chelsea answered. "Boys always mess up the curve."

"And not enough crazies to qualify for the funny farm. I'm Jillian Longado. I'm sixteen, was born and raised in Texas"—she placed her hand over her heart in reverence—"and I can't wait for these fancy doctors to find me a new heart and a set of lungs so I can get on with my life."

"You need *both?*" Chelsea blurted out, then wished she'd used more restraint.

Jillian didn't seem to notice. "Actually, that's three organs. One heart and two lungs. How about you?"

"Just one heart."

They laughed together as the absurdity of their situations hit them. Chelsea noticed that Jillian had a faint blue cast to her lips and that her finger-tips looked clubbed—a sign of oxygen depriva-tion. Jillian said, "My twin brother calls me the queen of hearts—and lungs, and lungs." She made a rolling motion with her hand. "He says that so long as they're transplanting, maybe I could get a new brain too. You got a brother?"

"No, I'm an only."

"I have two grown sisters, then along came me and my twin, DJ—that stands for Douglas Jed. He also always says I talk too much. What do you think?"

Chelsea couldn't help smiling. "You remind me of a friend I once had. She was real talkative too, but Amanda was from Kansas. You know, like Dorothy in the *Wizard of Oz*."

"I've heard of Kansas. I think Daddy tried to buy it once." Jillian's eyes twinkled. "My folks own a big cattle ranch outside of Dallas, and Daddy's pretty used to getting what he wants. That's why it's real bothersome to him that I need these organs and he can't do anything about it except wait."

"Have you been sick for long?" Chelsea asked, glad that the ability to pay was never a factor in who got organs. Her family wasn't rich, as Jillian's obviously was, and so they'd never have been able to pay for her to receive a new heart. Even Katie's Wish money hadn't been able to buy her heart.

"Just since I was born," Jillian said.

"Me too," Chelsea confessed.

"It didn't happen to DJ. Just me. It's called Eisenmenger's syndrome. The doctors operated on me once, but it didn't do much good. My heart's too big on one side, and that's put a terrible strain on my lungs. And even though the doctors have got me stabilized with fistfuls of medicines, I've been sent here to wait around for someone who's about my size and has my blood type to kick off so I can get a new set of inside plumbing."

"You act pretty cheerful about it." The flip, irreverent way Jillian discussed her problems amazed Chelsea.

Jillian looked thoughtful before saying, "Well, I can't change it. And I'm all cried out about it. I guess the only thing to do is go with the flow and make the best of it."

"Where are you staying while you wait to be transplanted?"

"Daddy's got me and Mama a suite at a hotel downtown. How about you? You live around here?"

Quickly, Chelsea told Jillian about Katie and their friendship.

"You mean, Katie's actually living proof that this transplantation stuff works?"

"Living and thriving proof."

"Can I meet her?"

Chelsea considered the request. "I guess so. She's really special."

"How about if the two of you come to my hotel and we can visit and eat."

It seemed like a good idea. "I'll ask Katie tonight. She could drive us over."

"Don't bother. I'll have a limo sent for you. Just let's arrange a time."

Taken aback, Chelsea said, "That would be cool."

Jillian shuffled back to her seat in the auditorium and fumbled in her purse. "Here's my phone number." She wrote the name of her hotel and her number on a business-size card of baby pink embossed with her name in gold letters and gave it to Chelsea.

Chelsea was impressed that a girl would have her very own name cards. "I'll call you," Chelsea promised, tucking the card into her pocket.

The auditorium door swung open, and Dr. Cummings entered, along with a small army of doctors and psychologists. Chelsea smiled and settled in the seat beside Jillian, suddenly feeling happier than she had felt in days.

That night, when Katie came by, Chelsea sat up in bed, put aside her book, and told Katie all about her new friend. Then she showed her the card.

"I'm impressed," Katie said. "I've never met any really rich people. She's not a snob?"

"No way. She's a regular person. Really nice. Can you imagine needing a heart *and* lungs? It made me feel lucky to only be needing a heart."

"No matter how bad off we think we are, there's always somebody worse off."

"You know what I was just thinking? Maybe we could find a way for Jillian to visit Jenny House. Even with all her money, she's probably never seen anyplace like it."

Katie looked hesitant.

"Jenny House is for people like Jillian. For people like us. Remember, Mr. Holloway said we had standing invitations to come whenever we wanted."

"I guess we can write Mr. Holloway and ask. But I want to meet this Jillian for myself."

"I could see if Saturday's all right with her."

"Josh and I have a date for Saturday night."

"Saturday afternoon's open, isn't it?"

"I was supposed to go to the library and start on a research paper for English lit."

"Please?"

"A limo?"

"It'll come right to our door."

Katie offered an exaggerated sigh. "Oh, well, if you're going to twist my arm this way."

"Great! I'll call Jillian tomorrow and ask her if Saturday's okay with her."

Katie stood. "I need to crack some books, and you need to rest. You look tired."

"All I do is rest," Chelsea grumbled, but she was feeling weary. She peered up at Katie. "Is something bothering you?"

Katie started. "Of course not. Why do you ask?"

"You've seemed a little preoccupied lately. Like something's on your mind."

"Nothing special. Just school and all the work I have to get done."

Chelsea's eyes narrowed. "You sure there's nothing else? Remember who you're talking to—the girl with intuition. Wasn't I the one who first noticed Amanda's crush on Jeff this summer?"

"How can I forget? Really, everything's fine with me."

"It's not my being here?"

"Oh, no," Katie answered.

"You'd tell me if something was going on at

school with you? You know how I love to live vicariously."

Katie laughed and breezed toward the doorway. "Don't worry. All's well."

Just before Katie stepped into the hallway, Chelsea playfully called, "It's a good thing you already have a boyfriend, or I'd have to give you the third degree."

Katie didn't glance backward. Chelsea watched her leave, but noticed a slight stiffening of her friend's back. She wondered at Katie's reaction. If Katie wanted to share secrets with her, she would.

Chelsea turned off her bedside lamp and thought about spending the day with Jillian until she fell into a dreamless sleep.

Four

Katie walked into the public library Friday night and allowed herself one nervous glance about the room. She hoped with all her heart that Garrison wouldn't be in the library tonight. She proceeded directly to a study table in the farmost corner behind the reference book stacks.

"We should get started on our paper," he'd told her on Wednesday following class. "I'm helping my dad shape up our yard Saturday morning, but I'll be free later in the day."

"I can start the project without you," Katie said.

"But that's the problem. I don't want you to start without me. I want to be with you. Even if it's for some dumb class project."

The way he looked at her left her with a feeling of lightheadedness she couldn't explain. Or ignore. She told herself he was just some guy putting moves on her, but the logic of her arguments didn't make her feel less attracted to him. *Keep away*, she insisted silently. That was her only safe recourse.

On Thursday, she'd coolly informed him that she would start the project without him on Saturday, although she knew she'd be spending the day with Chelsea at Jillian's hotel. She felt her cheeks redden when she lied, but hoped he didn't notice.

Katie settled behind the stacks, arranged her notebook and note cards, and went to the card catalog to look up basic information on the topic she and Garrison had been assigned: "The Role of Evil in Shakespeare's *Othello*." She was busily taking notes when she heard a male voice say, "Hello, partner. I didn't expect to find you here."

She almost dropped her pencil, mustered her composure, and told Garrison, "Something came up for tomorrow."

"Good. Then we can get started tonight." The way he said it, the way his eyes appraised her, made her wonder if his words didn't hold a double meaning.

"You take these references," she said, handing him the sources she'd scribbled on a piece of notebook paper. "I'll get others."

He nodded and sauntered toward the stacks. She took several deep breaths and turned her attention back to the card catalog. Later, when she returned to her table, Garrison was already seated, poring over several volumes. He looked up as she sat opposite him. "There's not much here," he said.

"Sure there is. We just have to find the right angle."

He studied her. "Do you want an A on this project?" His question sounded challenging.

"Yes. My grades are important, what with college and all."

"My grades are important to me too. That's why I think we need to go the extra mile."

"How do you mean?"

"I think we should do our research at the University of Michigan library. I can get access because my father's faculty. That library will have reference material this place never even heard of."

His plan sounded like a winner to Katie, and she said so.

"Good," he said. "That means we'll have to go together. How's Monday night? I'll pick you up." His smile was quick and disarming.

Katie felt as if she'd been bamboozled. As if he'd already mapped out an agenda and she'd unwittingly agreed to it. She remembered the cool, casual way Lacey had handled Jeff over the summer. Lacey had feigned indifference to the point where Jeff had been left totally in the dark about her actual feelings for him. But Katie knew that she herself wasn't cool and collected like Lacey. She was slow and scattered and not very skillful in dealing with the opposite sex. "I'm not sure," she told Garrison. "I have other things going on."

He cocked his head, as if waiting for her explanation.

Josh's image floated in her memory. "You know I have a boyfriend," she began slowly.

"I've heard. Martel, isn't it?" She nodded, and Garrison flashed another smile. "You didn't think I was coming on to you, did you?" He chuckled. "Look, you're a pretty girl, Katie, but I'm not into snaking away another guy's girl. You're one of the few people I've met who've been nice to me, and so, of course, I want to return the favor. I think getting an A on our lit project is the least I can do."

Katie felt her face flush hot and knew she was turning red with embarrassment. Had she drawn the completely wrong conclusions about his attentions? "Well, I want an A also. I only mentioned Josh because he and I spend a lot of time together."

"Are you saying that you have to check with him before you can go research a paper for school?"

His phrasing made it sound as if she were some kind of puppet and Josh were pulling her strings. "No!" she insisted. "Josh and I aren't like that. We have an understanding."

"What kind of understanding?"

How could Garrison twist her words and make it sound as if she had less than a mind of her own? "You don't understand, and I don't have time to explain it. It's complicated, that's all."

"Then, if it's cool with your boyfriend, I'd like to take you to the UM library Monday night so we can ace this paper. What's complicated about that?"

"Nothing, I guess."

"So it's settled. We have a study date for Monday night." Garrison stood and scooped up his notebook. "And right now, I don't see any reason to waste my time in this library. So, I'll say goodbye, have a great weekend, and I'll see you in class on Monday morning."

He was gone before Katie could open her mouth. She sat, dumbstruck, feeling as if she'd somehow lost control of a situation she didn't understand. All she knew was that at this moment, she wanted to be with Josh. He was kind and caring and gentle. *And I love him*, she reminded herself.

Katie left the library and drove straight to Josh's grandfather's house, where she knew Josh would be waiting for her.

"Is this car neat or what?" Chelsea slid open a compartment door in the console of the limo and peered inside. "Hey, Katie, there's a TV set in here."

"And there's food to feed an army," Katie said, opening a small refrigerator embedded under the seat cushion.

The plush velour seats faced each other in the back of the expensive car. Chelsea sat opposite Katie, who poked through the contents of the refrigerator. "Want a soda?" Katie asked. "Or a sandwich?"

Outside, traffic was light on the expressway taking them downtown. Chelsea could barely see the back of the driver's head through the smoked glass partition. "Nothing for me. Do you think that guy can hear us?"

"Probably not," Katie replied, pointing to a row of buttons. "I think this is an intercom that allows us to talk to him if we want. Should we buzz him?"

Chelsea snatched Katie's finger, poised over a button. "Don't you dare! What would we say?"

"We could ask him if he has any mustard."

Chelsea giggled. "Boy, I wonder what it's like to be this rich?"

"Jenny Crawford was rich," Katie said. Chelsea nodded, recalling the portrait of the beautiful young girl that hung over the stone fireplace at Jenny House. "If I had money, I'd give it away just like she did," Katie continued. "I'd make huge donations to research. I'd fly all my friends in for a weekend at Jenny House. I'd buy everybody I liked a present."

"Would you buy me my own virtual reality game?"

Katie snapped her fingers. "In a heartbeat."

"Speaking of heartbeats . . ." Chelsea placed her hand over her heart. "I wish you could buy me one and skip all this transplant waiting."

Katie smiled wistfully. "I used to wish the same thing."

The limo pulled up into the curving brick archway of a giant hotel. A doorman opened the car door, and Katie stepped out first. A wheelchair had been brought for Chelsea.

"I don't want that," Chelsea said when she saw it. "I can walk."

The doorman nodded and led the way through a mammoth lobby that gleamed with brass and mirrors. Giant floral arrangements scented the air, and soft music playing on a piano and harp gave the hotel a feeling of splendid elegance. Chelsea walked past an indoor pond where lily pads floated alongside pale pink lotus blossoms. Bright golden fish languished beneath the water's surface.

The doorman took them to what seemed to be a private elevator, and when the door slid open, he said, "This goes express to the penthouse. Miss Longado is waiting for you."

Katie exchanged glances with Chelsea and mouthed *Miss Longado?* Chelsea shrugged. Alone in the elevator, the two girls suppressed giggles and grabbed each other's hands. The elevator, lined in marble and mirrors, floated upward so smoothly that the only sensation Chelsea felt was a slight fluttering in her stomach. The movement stopped, and the doors slid open.

A woman dressed in a gray uniform smiled warmly at Chelsea and Katie. "Hello. Miss Jillian is in her room waiting for you. Follow me."

Five

THERE WAS NO way Chelsea could act indifferent as the maid led her and Katie through the spacious penthouse.

The maid ushered them into a bedroom that was at least the size of three bedrooms from Katie's house put together. In the center of the room was an elevated platform, and on it, an enormous bed, where Jillian lay. An oxygen tank stood beside the bed, and a thin tube led from the tank to Jillian's nostrils. She waved the girls over to her bedside. "Sorry about this, but my lungs need a little extra help today."

Understanding fully, Chelsea brushed aside the apology and introduced Katie.

"Chelsea says you've had a transplant," Jillian said. Her words sounded breathy, and her Texas drawl was quite distinctive. "Is that true? You sure look regular."

Katie laughed, feeling a wave of pity and camaraderie with the bedridden girl. "Two years ago, I looked just like you do now—all hooked up to tanks of oxygen."

"But a new heart changed all that," Chelsea inserted, eager to make Jillian feel at ease.

Jillian's skin looked pale, but her eyes were bright with curiosity. "Chelsea says she's living with you until she gets a donor. She's lucky. I sure miss my home."

Katie surveyed the room. "Well, my house is nothing like this. That's for sure."

"Katie's home is perfect," Chelsea insisted. "Having Katie is better than having a sister, because we never argue."

"A *poor* sister," Katie joked.

"This is the main bedroom," Jillian explained, sounding almost apologetic. "My folks made me take it so I'd be comfortable. Actually, it reminds me of a barn back at the ranch. Mama's taken one of the smaller rooms, and most weekends Daddy flies in and stays with us. He should be here from the airport any minute now with my brother, DJ. I want you to meet my family. You'll like them."

There was a knock on the door, and when it opened, three people trooped inside. A man, obviously Jillian's dad, filled the room with his presence. He looked suntanned and ruddy, and wore a cowboy hat and boots; his belt buckle was ornately carved silver. He went swiftly to Jillian's bed and hugged her. "How's my princess doing?" he asked in a booming voice.

Jillian insisted he not make a fuss and introduced him to Katie and Chelsea. Jillian's mother was a pretty woman with blond hair and blue eyes. Chelsea noticed on her hands several diamond rings that reminded her of boulders. Jillian's brother was blond, tall, and muscular, a picture of an outdoorsman with cowboy good looks. Chelsea could hardly take her eyes off him.

He swept his black hat off his head and said, "Glad to meet you."

Chelsea's pulse raced. She saw the resemblance between Jillian and DJ through their eyes and along their jawlines. The main difference between them lay in DJ's robust good health and Jillian's lack of it. The difference was even more pronounced when DJ bent and kissed his sister.

"Nice to see you could tear yourself away from Shelby to come and see me," Jillian said with a jab to DJ's chest.

"What've you got against Shelby?" DJ asked, his blue eyes mischievous. "She's fine, and she thinks highly of you."

Jillian made a face and looked to Chelsea and Katie. "Shelby's dumb as a brick. I don't know why he wastes his time on her."

"I don't think it's her brain that appeals to me," DJ said.

His father laughed, and his mother hooked her arm through his. "None of that kind of talk,

Douglas. You mind your mouth around Jillian's company."

Chelsea was startled by the open, easy banter among Jillian's family. She'd never heard parents talk to their kids as if they were equals. Katie was looking amused, so Chelsea figured she wasn't offended by them. Jillian said, "Tell me everything that's going on at home."

Her mother pulled at Jillian's dad and said, "Let these kids visit. I'll go make arrangements for lunch. You all will join us, won't you?"

Katie and Chelsea nodded acceptance. When their parents were gone, Jillian grabbed DJ's hand and said, "How's my horse? You exercising him?"

"Shelby and I went riding yesterday."

"You let that girl on Windsong? How could you?"

DJ chucked her under her chin. "I rode Windsong."

Mollified, Jillian settled back against her pillows. Chelsea could tell that the exertion had cost her strength, because Jillian closed her eyes and sucked oxygen. Chelsea saw a shadow cross DJ's face, momentary and fleeting, like clouds shifting across the sun. The look disappeared almost as quickly as it had come.

DJ held his sister's hand and said to Chelsea and Katie, "I'm glad Jillian's made some friends."

"We're in the transplant program together," Chelsea explained, suddenly feeling a need to fill in the silence left by Jillian's lassitude. "I need a heart. Katie's already gotten a transplant."

"You don't say." DJ studied Katie with renewed interest.

"She already has a boyfriend," Jillian said from the depths of her pillows without opening her eyes.

Chelsea felt a twinge of envy because DJ obviously had noticed Katie and not her.

"That cuts," DJ replied, acting offended. "I'm curious, that's all. I don't make a pass at every pretty girl I see, you know."

"We were wombmates, remember? I know exactly how you think."

"Well, if all you're going to do is insult me, I'm going to leave the three of you to yourselves."

"Is that a threat or a promise?" Jillian opened one eye and studied her brother playfully.

DJ stood and, picking up his hat, walked to the door. "If you're lucky, I'll join you for lunch."

"Thanks for the favor. We'll try to contain ourselves."

Chelsea saw the affection in Jillian's face for her brother and again experienced a twist of envy. How lonely she had been, growing up a sick, only child. For all her health problems, Jillian was lucky to have the kind of family she did.

When the three of them were alone, Jillian asked, "So, what do you think of my family?"

"I don't think I've ever met anybody like them," Katie said with a laugh.

"They are pretty special, aren't they?" Jillian motioned for Katie and Chelsea to sit on the bed with her. "I wish I could have been healthy like DJ. It's been awfully hard on him. He's perfectly fine, and I'm not, even though we have the same parents."

"And you were wombmates," Chelsea added, taken by the idea that Jillian and DJ were twins.

"Yeah, go figure. Same DNA, but in me, the stuff goes crazy." A brief, awkward silence fell. Jillian finally cleared her throat and looked to Katie. "So, you've had a heart transplant. Tell me about it. I want the truth. Not this medical stuff the doctors keep feeding me. They can quote more dumb statistics, but not *tell* a person one real thing about how things actually are!"

"I'll do better than that," Katie said, glancing around the room to make sure they were alone and that DJ had shut the bedroom door securely behind him. "I'll show you."

Katie pulled her shirttail from her jeans and undid the buttons. Slowly, she parted the material and exposed her chest. A long, straight scar, raised and slightly red, stretched under her bra from the center of her breastbone to her belly button. "Eventually, it'll get thinner and turn white," she explained, "but this is proof that they filleted me like a chicken, pulled out all my old stuffing, and put in new."

Jillian's eyes grew wide with wonder. Even Chelsea was moved by the sight, for although she'd spent the entire summer with Katie, she'd never seen the whole scar this way.

"Can I touch it?" Jillian asked.

Katie leaned closer, and Jillian gingerly ran her fingers along the ridged skin.

"Is that what they're going to do to me and Chelsea?"

"Yes," Katie said. "Out with the old. In with the new."

"It's kind of scary."

"I know. I was scared too. And the first time I saw this wound, with all the sutures, I freaked out. They had to give me tranquilizers to calm me down. I felt like a Frankenstein monster."

"Well, it's really weird to think someone can trade your heart for another," Jillian replied. "Like you're made up of assorted, interchangeable body parts."

"Parts is parts," Katie said with a flip of her hand. "Seriously, it's no picnic, but it's worth it. I'm living proof of that."

"I wonder what my chances are," Jillian mused. "I mean, I need lungs too."

"They wouldn't have put you on the beeper if they didn't think you were a good candidate," Katie assured her.

Jillian turned toward Chelsea. "I'm glad you're waiting with me. I'm glad we're in the therapy group together and glad you brought Katie to talk to me. It makes me feel less like some medical freak."

Chelsea nodded. "We're in this together, all right."

When it was time to eat lunch, Jillian's dad picked her up and carried her out to a chair at a table overlooking a balcony high above the city. A waiter served food from a cart, and when he stepped aside, DJ raised his glass of cola to the three girls. "Here's to new hearts. And new friends."

Chelsea felt secure about the "friends" part of DJ's words. She liked Jillian immensely and could tell that Katie liked her too. But the "new hearts" part left her frightened. One day, her beeper would go off, and the doctors would cut out her heart! She could hardly think about it without feeling nauseated. She didn't want to let the others know. She didn't want them to see her fear. She smiled broadly because she was afraid she'd faint and they'd realize just what a coward Chelsea James really was.

Six

Dear Chelsea,

So, you and Katie have gone and gotten yourselves a new friend! I'm wounded. All right, maybe just jealous. Even though I'm back in school in a big way, and even though all my friends are still around, I feel like an outsider. I know it's the crummy diabetes that sets me apart. Of course, I never talk about it to my friends . . . what with perfection being one of the highest criteria for social acceptance around Miami High.

My parents badgered me into attending a diabetes support group. I hate it! Not a cute guy in the bunch. But that's not my real problem. It's the sitting around and revealing the secrets of your soul to strangers that gets to me. Why should I spill my guts to kids I don't even care about? It's not like this summer with you and Katie and Mandy. (Not that I talked about this stupid disease much with you all, but at least I didn't feel like a specimen or a lab experiment.)

On the home front, things have gone steadily downhill. It's like a war zone at my house. Dad and Mom hardly speak, and then only to argue. What's the matter with them? Don't they know how this is tearing me up? It's barely October, and I'm already worried about the holidays. How are we ever going to make it through?

Excuse me. I don't mean to unload on you. I know waiting around for some transplant operation can't be a picnic. The one thing I'm looking forward to is the school play coming up in the spring. I've signed on to do makeup. (Especially on the male lead—Todd Larson. Really cool guy!)

Believe it or not, there are times I wish I was back at Jenny House. I know I groused tons about the place when I was there, but looking back, I see it was a pretty special place. Remember your promise for us all to meet there next summer. (Don't let me down!) As for Jeff, yes, he's written me and called, but I won't answer his letters, and I cut him off on the phone. I refuse to get involved with some guy who's got hemophilia. All I want is to party and have fun and forget about sick people! (Present company excluded, of course.)

So, share this letter with Katie, and know that I'm pulling for you. You have Katie call me the

minute *you get beeped and go in for your transplant. And tell that Jillian girl hello for me. If you
two like her, then I will too. I promise I'll be nice
to her.*

*Bye for now,
Lacey*

Chelsea put down Lacey's letter when she finished reading it aloud to Katie and said, "Do you
notice anything different about Lacey?"

Katie shrugged. "Sounds like our same old
friend to me . . . refusing to deal with reality."

"I think she sounds desperate."

"If you mean about her parents—"

Chelsea fluttered her fingers impatiently. "More
than her parents. It's like everything in her life is
falling apart."

"You got *that* out of this letter?"

"I'm reading between the lines. I think she's in
bad shape. Sure, in the letter she comes across as
only annoyed, but I'm telling you, it goes deeper
than that." Chelsea stabbed at the paper with her
finger. "There's an unwritten volume here about
'perfection' and 'social acceptance.' And what
about this Todd guy? Since when has Lacey let on
that any guy appeals to her?"

Katie shook her head. "You're the one with the
ESP, Chelsea, so if you say so, I believe you. But so
what if it's true? What can we do about it? Until
Lacey wants to face reality, how can anyone help
her?"

"Jeff could help, if she'd let him. The guy is crazy about her."

"Forget it. I fought that battle all summer. Trying to run interference between Jeff and Lacey and Amanda almost did me in."

"But Amanda's gone now," Chelsea said quietly.

The cold reality of that sad fact couldn't be forgotten. All at once, Katie jumped up. "I've got to go. Josh is dropping me by the UM library so that I can work on my lit paper."

"Is he getting used to your studying so much with Garrison?"

"Hardly," Katie said, pulling Chelsea's brush through her thick black hair. "But the whole thing is harmless, so Josh is just being paranoid for no reason."

"No reason?" Chelsea asked.

Katie felt self-conscious and turned away from Chelsea. "Now, don't go trying to psychoanalyze me the way you do everybody else. There's nothing to analyze."

Chelsea arched her eyebrow. "Really? So, then why is your face turning red?"

"I could wait out here in the parking lot for you to finish," Josh said, pulling his car to a halt in the lot nearest the University of Michigan's gigantic library.

"It's cold out here. You'll freeze." Katie gathered her books and prepared to get out of the car.

"How much longer before you finish this paper anyway?"

"Another few weeks. The basic research is almost over, then we'll just have to write the thing." She kept her voice light, as if the process were an annoyance. In truth, the paper was driving her nuts. Not the paper. Spending so much time with Garrison.

She reached for the door handle. "Look, I'll call you the minute I get home tonight."

"Garrison taking you home?"

"What do you expect me to do, Josh? Call a cab?" She could tell that her retort stung him, so she tried a different tack. "Josh, you know how much I want to qualify for a track scholarship, but running isn't enough to get me one like it once might have done. Coaches want competitive runners, but they also want good students. I lost a whole year of my life with my operation and all. I'm not the best anymore out on the track."

"You're still good, Katie. I know how hard you train. By this spring when track season starts, you'll be unbeatable."

"You have more faith in me than I do," she said with a laugh. She sobered and with intensity added, "I want good grades. I want to *earn* that scholarship. Acing honors English would mean a lot to me. It's a top priority in my life right now."

"There was a time when I was a top priority in your life," Josh said softly.

Guilt tore at her. Still, she clenched her teeth and tried not to overreact. "You still are."

"But not quite as high as studying with Garrison."

"It bothers me when you don't trust me."

"Garrison bothers *me*. He's cocky and a show-off, and I've seen the way he looks at you."

"This conversation is silly, and it's going no place." Katie jerked open the door. "I'll call you later." She slammed the door and hurried up the sidewalk. She heard Josh gun the engine and squeal out of the parking lot. The smell of burned rubber hung in the night air. She sagged on the steps of the brightly lit library, torn between going in and facing Garrison and going to a pay phone and calling Josh to come back for her.

Then, remembering what she'd told Josh about the importance of her grades, Katie gathered her ragged emotions and went inside. She found Garrison on the fourth floor, back in a corner near a window. He waved as she approached. "You look unhappy," Garrison said.

The last thing she wanted was for him to suspect that there was tension between her and Josh. "It's been a long day," she replied, dumping her books and taking the chair across from his.

"Want to talk about it?"

"No."

He shrugged and turned an open magazine toward her. "I think this article is good. It discusses Iago's lack of motivation for hating Othello, and this scholar thinks it weakens Shakespeare's whole play. Without motivation, Iago's hatred seems pointless."

She tried to focus on what Garrison was telling her. He was a brilliant thinker and as intent on scoring big on this paper as she was. He'd told her he was aiming for entering Harvard and after earning an undergraduate degree there would apply to the law school. "I guess motives count," Katie said.

She hated it when he looked at her as if he could see inside her thoughts. "Did you have words with the boyfriend?" he asked.

She bristled. "Why would you assume Josh and I are having problems? There's nothing wrong between us."

A sly smile flicked the corners of Garrison's mouth. "You're a lousy liar, Katie."

Flustered, she stood and, without meaning to, tipped her chair over. "You have no right—"

He was beside her in an instant, took her hands in his, and tugged her toward him. "Calm down before they throw us out. Come on. I'll take you to the student union and buy you a soda." He began to lead her to the interior lobby and elevators.

"But our books and stuff—"

"Will be fine till we get back."

She said nothing, allowing him to take her out of the main entrance and into the night. *I shouldn't go*, she told herself. For weeks, he'd treated her with friendly indifference—ever since the time she'd insisted she had a boyfriend and he'd acted surprised that she'd think he'd move in on her. She'd seen him with other girls around school. Part of her had been glad. But another part of her had reacted.

Garrison drove to the student union without a word, and once they were inside the room where students gathered for coffee and visiting, he found them a booth, brought back two colas and an order of fries, and sat down next to her.

She moved into the corner because his thigh was touching hers. He jabbed his straw into his cup, turned to her, and said, "So, what's going on, Katie? What's got you so wound up?"

Seven

WITHOUT WARNING, TEARS filled Katie's eyes. Garrison didn't say a word, only handed her a napkin. She dabbed at the moisture, hating herself for allowing Garrison to see her in such a state of muddled confusion. "I have a lot of pressure on me," she said lamely.

"But your boyfriend is a part of it, isn't he? He doesn't like us spending so much time together."

She peered at Garrison, and something in his expression told her more was going on than he was telling her. "Has Josh said something to you?"

"He cornered me in the gym the other day. He said some things. Made some suggestions about what might happen if I didn't butt out of your life."

"What things?" Katie felt shocked and mortified.

This wasn't like Josh at all. Josh was kind and sweet. He wouldn't threaten anyone.

"Look, Katie, it was just between us guys. Don't worry. I wasn't intimidated."

"If things were said about me, then it's between all of us. I can't believe what you're telling me."

Garrison's hand reached out and closed over hers. "He's in love, Katie. I understand why he said what he did. How long have the two of you been involved anyway?"

Josh had no right to manipulate her life this way. No right to decide who she could see or not see. Suddenly, her pounding heart reminded her of Josh's role in her life. Fresh tears pooled in her eyes.

"Katie," Garrison whispered. "Please tell me what's going on. I think I have the right to know."

She told him the story, haltingly at first, then with more intensity. She told him about her illness and her need for a transplant, about Aaron's death and how Josh had figured out who'd received his brother's heart. She told him about Gramps, Josh's alcoholic parents, her own parents' affection for Josh. She told him about the Transplant Games and her footrace and Josh's role in her training. She finished with her hopes of a track scholarship and even a mention of Chelsea and how Katie needed to be there for her friend as she faced a similar transplant procedure.

When she was finished, she leaned back in the booth, drained, but also purged. It had felt good to unburden herself. Garrison's intense gaze never left her face, and for a moment she thought she might drown in the depths of his incredible brown eyes. "Well, I'll have to admit, Katie, I've never heard anything like this before in my life."

"It isn't something you walk around talking about. There are kids at school who know the basic facts, but they have their own lives to live, so no one thinks about me and my problems. Besides, I've never wanted anyone gossiping about me."

"It explains why Josh is so protective of you. There's *you*, of course. But there's also a piece of his brother living inside you."

"That's true. So, now can you see how complicated things are between me and Josh? He means a lot to me. He's given me so much."

Garrison sighed and stood. "Come on. Let's go back to the library."

"I can't think about the paper tonight," she confessed.

"Me either. We'll get our stuff, and I'll take you home."

The trip back to the library, the collection of their books, and the drive to Katie's house was a long, silent journey. Katie could tell that Garrison was deep in thought, and for a while, she wondered if she'd done the right thing dumping her life story on him. She was feeling uneasy and a bit disloyal to Josh. But he shouldn't have done what he did by confronting Garrison.

When Garrison stopped his car at Katie's house,

she fumbled for the door handle. He caught her arm. "Wait."

Slowly, she turned toward him. He raised her chin with his forefinger. "I'm glad you told me what you did, Katie. I see now that your involvement with Josh is far more complex than most relationships. Of course, it's up to you, but I'd rather you not tell Josh I said anything to you about his and my discussion in the gym. I know he won't come after me, and there's no reason for the two of you to have a fight over it."

She nodded, feeling her heart—Aaron's heart—thudding in her chest. "W-we still have the paper to finish," she said. "I want to complete it . . . regardless of Josh."

"All right." Garrison smoothed her hair, ran his fingers through its thickness, and caught it in his palm. "I want you to think about something for me."

"What?"

"I've only known you a short while, but I heard all you said tonight. I want you to think long and hard about your feelings for Josh."

"I love him," she replied quickly.

Garrison ran his thumb down the length of her jaw, making shivers race up her spine. "He saved your life," Garrison said, as if she'd not spoken. "That's a big debt, Katie. But I want you to consider what you really feel toward him. Is it love or gratitude?"

* * *

Chelsea picked up the Chance card and read, " 'Go directly to jail. Do not pass Go. Do not collect two hundred dollars.' " She squealed and placed her Monopoly game piece in the block marked "Jail."

"What are you complaining about?" Jillian said. "I'm the one who's broke. Look, I've just landed on Boardwalk, and I can't even afford to buy it."

"That breaks my heart."

The two girls were sitting in the middle of Jillian's huge bed, the Monopoly board spread out between them. A room service cart loaded with sodas, desserts, and snack foods stood by the bed. Chelsea picked up the dice, jiggled them in her hand, and studied them closely. "You know," she remarked, "I don't think I've ever played a game of Monopoly quite like this one. Houses made out of real silver, hotels made from gold, brass game pieces—are these dice some kind of gemstone?"

"Garnets," Jillian answered, shrugging her shoulders apologetically. "Daddy's idea. He had the set specially made for me. He gets a little carried away sometimes, but he means well."

Chelsea laughed. "Seems like a nice way to get carried away."

"He's always trying to make it up to me because I'm sick. Like he feels it's his and Mama's fault."

"How could it be?"

"Bad genetics," Jillian explained with another shrug. "Parents feel guilty sometimes. You know—responsible for the defects."

Jillian's explanation gave Chelsea pause. Had

her parents ever felt the same way? They'd never had other children. Was it because of fears they'd have another defective one? "But your folks had healthy kids too."

"They did. Three others. But Daddy's the type who remembers his mistakes, not his triumphs."

"But you all seem so close."

"We are. I love my family more than anything. They're always around for me. I've tried real hard to not be sick, to be well for them, but I just can't be. I'm hoping this transplant will change every-thing. I'm hoping that once it's over and I've re-covered, I can do all the things I want to do with them."

Jillian's enthusiasm toward getting the trans-plant only reminded Chelsea of her fear of it. Why couldn't she be eager and optimistic about it the way Jillian was? She asked, "So, what things would you do?"

Jillian tipped her head thoughtfully. "I'd go on a weeklong trail ride the way DJ does. I'd herd the cattle and sleep under the stars. Daddy loves his ranch, and he's made it plain that it will go to me and DJ when he dies. Our sisters all married rich, and they don't care much about the ranch any-way."

"So, once you get well, you'll become a cattle baron?"

"Baroness."

They giggled together and didn't hear the knock on the door, so DJ pushed it open and stuck his head inside the room. "Is that all you two have got to do?"

"I didn't say you could come in," Jillian announced.

"I didn't ask your permission," DJ countered good-naturedly, coming toward the bed.

Chelsea felt her heart skip a beat. She shifted on the bed self-consciously. Because of her heart problems, she'd not had much experience being with boys, but she knew when a guy was affecting her emotions. DJ was cute. Rugged-looking. Chelsea had met plenty of guys over the summer at Jenny House, but none of them had made her blood race the way DJ did.

"I thought you and Daddy were flying back to Texas this afternoon," Jillian said. It was Sunday, and because of school for DJ and obligations at the ranch for their father, their visits were limited to weekends.

"We're taking off soon. Trying to get rid of me? So tell me, Chelsea, is that nice of my sister?"

Chelsea's mind went blank. "Uh—no," she said, and felt dumb.

"I'm shocked you even showed this weekend," Jillian needled. "Shocked that Shelby unhooked your chain and let you out of her sight."

"You're mean as a snake," DJ said with an impish grin. "Shelby had a cheerleading camp to go to this weekend."

"Why am I not surprised?"

"I don't know why I let you bad-mouth my girl this way." Jillian opened her mouth to retort, but

DJ covered it with his palm. "Don't say something you'll have to make up to me about." He bent and kissed her forehead. "Got you last," he said, backing away from the bed.

Jillian raised up on her knees and put her hands on her hips. "You coming next weekend?"

"Maybe. Would you miss me if I didn't?"

"Fat chance."

Chelsea watched the two of them give one another a long, clinging look, and realized how deep their affection for each other went. How scared each of them was of not seeing the other again.

"If they beep you—"

"Mama will call, and you and Daddy can be here in a few hours," Jillian replied. "Now, go on and get out of here. Chelsea and I have a game to finish."

"Don't let her cheat," DJ told Chelsea.

When he left, the room felt empty, as if it had somehow grown smaller. Chelsea saw a film of moisture in Jillian's eyes, and didn't know how to respond.

Jillian sniffed loudly, wiped the back of her hand over her eyes, turned toward Chelsea, and asked, "So, tell me, Chelsea James, how long have you had this crush on my brother?"

Eight

CHELSEA FELT HER face flush and grow hot with embarrassment. "What are you talking about?"

Jillian skewered her with a knowing look. "Don't play the innocent with me. It's written all over your face whenever DJ walks in a room."

"Honestly, that's just not true—"

Jillian pierced the air with a squeal. "Friends know what friends are thinking. And real friends don't deny the obvious."

Chelsea bowed her head guiltily. Jillian was right. What good did it do to deny what Jillian had already surmised? "Okay . . . so I've got this teensy-weensy little crush. But not to worry, he's safe enough from me. I'm sure he doesn't know I'm alive, what with his big romance with Shelby and all."

"Don't remind me. I'd much rather have him interested in a girl as special as you."

"You think I'm special?"

"I pick my friends real carefully. I liked you from the first minute I met you at that therapy session. And after we talked, I liked you even more. All my life, I've been the odd one, the sick one. People are sympathetic toward me, but no one really understands what it's like to be sick one hundred percent of the time."

"I know what you mean," Chelsea added. "Until I went to Jenny House this summer and met Katie and the others, I felt lonely and left out too. Everybody in the whole world seemed healthy except me. Kids on TV, in magazines—they're all the picture of glowing health."

"You got that right. If it weren't for telethons to raise money for some disease or other, the rest of the world would never think twice about people like us. Let's face it, our lives have never been normal. What I'm wondering is, if we get these transplants, will our lives be normal then?"

Chelsea pondered Jillian's question. "Katie seems normal," she said slowly. "But I know she can't be completely normal. There's stuff going on in her life she won't even talk about with me."

"What kind of stuff?"

"I'm not sure. But I feel that her transplant is somehow mixed up in it."

"But she's all right?"

"She's all right in the physical sense." Chelsea searched for a way to put her intuition into words.

"She's sort of at loose ends. Distracted. I can't explain it."

"Loose ends?" Jillian repeated. "Like unfinished business? You know, like your crush on DJ?"

Chelsea had hoped that Jillian had forgotten her earlier observation. "Your brother's a cute guy. I don't get to be around all that many. Plus, he's so sure of himself. And friendly."

Jillian blew air through pursed lips. "Well, if I had my way, he'd notice you instead of Shelby."

"I don't know this Shelby, but what have you got against her? You always seem down on her, and I know that you're really a caring person."

Jillian flashed Chelsea a look that said, *Sure-that's-me, Miss Nice-nice,* and both girls giggled. "Shelby's a real pain," Jillian said once they'd recovered from their giggle fit. "She treats me like I'm an untouchable."

"Explain."

"I guess there are people in the world who because they are physically perfect can't abide people who aren't. Shelby's one of them. She's a knockout in the looks department."

The information sent a sinking sensation through Chelsea's stomach. She recalled how pretty Lacey was, but even Lacey hadn't acted stuck-up about her beauty. Maybe because she had an incurable illness. Chelsea didn't know. "So, Shelby's drop-dead pretty. How does she treat you?"

"Like I'm some kind of freak. Oh, she's nice enough to my face when DJ's around, but the minute his back is turned, she's downright hateful. You'd think what I've got—bad heart and lungs—might be catching or something."

Chelsea saw that Jillian was trying to act as if Shelby's attitude only made her angry. But she could tell that although Jillian hid her feelings behind a mask of humor, she was hurt by Shelby's rejection. "She's ignorant, that's all."

"Don't you think I've tried to educate her? I really have tried to like this girl, Chelsea. She and DJ have been a twosome ever since we were in eighth grade together."

A quick calculation told Chelsea that DJ's romance with Shelby had been going on for three years. No simple little schooltime crush by that measure, she told herself.

Jillian continued. "I figured that if she meant that much to DJ, I should try to like her. But she's impossible to like."

"How so?"

Jillian dropped her head downward so that her thick head of red hair half hid her face. "I heard her making fun of me to some other girls. I was waiting by the gym after a football game. DJ plays on the high school team," she explained. "Anyway, I was standing sort of to one side in the shadows, and I heard Shelby imitating me for her friends . . . you know . . . the way I sound when I can't catch my breath, when I'm wheezing and trying not to black out because the pain is so bad."

Chelsea knew. Shelby's insensitivity made her

furious for Jillian's sake. "That's not right," she said.

"They laughed at her imitation. All those girls stood there and laughed, like it was one big joke. And Shelby went on and on making fun of me and making them laugh at me."

Jillian's hurt seemed real enough to touch. "Why didn't you tell DJ? I'll bet he would have broken up with her over it."

"He probably would have," Jillian agreed, raising her head. "But I won't stoop to her level. And besides, if I did, then their breakup would always be *my* fault instead of hers. And I want DJ to see her for what she really is and break off with her because of that, not because I tattled on her."

Chelsea wasn't sure she would have chosen such a course had it been her instead of Jillian, but she felt a growing respect toward Jillian because of her philosophy. "Hurting people just to get even isn't your style, is that what you're saying?"

Jillian grinned shyly. "I guess that's it. See, I knew you understood me."

"But what if DJ *doesn't* catch on?" Chelsea asked.

"Given enough time, he will." Jillian sounded ruefully confident and gave Chelsea a lopsided smile. "My daddy didn't raise a bunch of dummies."

Chelsea poked Jillian's arm playfully. "You're right. He didn't."

Jillian's eyes locked with Chelsea's. In that instant, Chelsea felt totally connected with her. The two of them might be sick, but at that moment, Chelsea felt she'd never known anybody like Jillian Longado, and she realized that never would she know anybody like her again.

Jillian broke the connection by clearing her throat and asking, "You tell me all the time about this Jenny House and what fun you had there. I think maybe I should check the place out. What do you think?"

"I told Katie the same thing," Chelsea exclaimed. "You'd really like Jenny House. There's no place else like it." Chelsea's face clouded momentarily. "The only problem I see is getting there. Katie thinks our doctors at the transplant program would give us a few days to go away, so long as we're attached to our beepers."

"Wouldn't that be a trauma," Jillian said. "Just our luck to be off on vacation and have our beepers go off."

"So, I guess that may be a problem. Jenny House is in North Carolina—that's a long drive by car." Chelsea was remembering when Josh had driven down from Michigan to surprise Katie. He'd driven almost around the clock.

"By car?" Jillian wrinkled her nose. "Who goes by car? We'll fly down."

Chelsea wasn't so sure her parents could afford such a weekend excursion for her. Nor was she certain Katie would be able to spend money on such a trip either. Still, it would be so much fun to show Jenny House to Jillian. The virtual reality games, the room where she'd spent the summer, the portrait of Jenny, maybe even the mountain plateau that held the makeshift memorial to Amanda. "Flying's expensive," Chelsea hedged.

"So, who cares?"

"You can't pay for all of us," Chelsea said. "I mean, that's *too* much to ask."

"So, who's going to pay commercial rates? We'll use Daddy's plane."

Dumbstruck, Chelsea stared, open-mouthed. "Your father has his own plane?"

"Of course. How do you think he and DJ get here from Texas most every weekend? They don't depend on commercial flights."

A laugh started down in Chelsea's throat and bubbled to the surface. "Your own plane. Why am I not surprised?" She used one of Jillian's favorite phrases.

"You're starting to sound like me—get help," Jillian said with a giggle.

"I've never known anyone with her own plane. And her own gold-plated Monopoly game."

"I told you that we do things in a big way in Texas."

"I think Katie should be the one to call Mr. Holloway—he's the director at Jenny House—and find out if we can come."

"*If?*" Jillian asked, arching an eyebrow. "We'd better get to go. If he gives us any trouble, I might have to do something drastic."

"Like what?"

"I just might have to have Daddy buy the place for me."

Chelsea collapsed in a fit of laughter. "You'd do that, wouldn't you?"

"I would." Jillian's blue eyes twinkled. "And who knows? For a really good friend, I just might be willing to throw in my brother as a booby prize."

Nine

❦

It was decided that the girls would visit Jenny House over Thanksgiving weekend. Chelsea's father came for turkey and all the trimmings at Katie's house on Thanksgiving Day, and early on Friday morning, when most of the country headed for the malls to officially begin Christmas shopping, Katie, Chelsea, and Jillian went to the airport, where Mr. Longado had his private jet fueled and waiting for the trip to North Carolina.

Chelsea could tell that all three sets of parents were nervous about the trip, but Jillian's dad had arranged to send a private nurse with them, and that made the anxious goodbyes less traumatic. The head of the transplant program had given his blessings for the trip, reminding them that because of the private jet, Jillian and Chelsea could easily be brought home should a potential donor be found.

When the girls were at last settled into their seats and the jet was taxiing down the runway for takeoff, Chelsea breathed a sigh of relief and gave a thumbs-up signal to her friends. Jillian smiled and leaned back against the seat. Chelsea thought Jillian looked tired and recognized the bluish cast on her lips as a sign that she was working for each breath. Every so often throughout the flight, the nurse took blood pressures, and offered Jillian oxygen, which made her breathing easier.

The plane was met at the Asheville airport by Richard Holloway himself. He hugged Katie and Chelsea, shook Jillian's hand, and gave her a hearty welcome. As they walked the hundred yards to his car, parked with special permission to the side of the runway, Jillian whispered, "He's good-looking. For an older guy, that is."

At the car, a blond girl threw open the door and bounced out. "Lacey!" Chelsea cried, throwing her arms around her. "No one told me you'd be here."

Chelsea looked at Katie, who shrugged innocently. "Surprise," Katie said.

Lacey's smile lit up her face. "I asked Katie to keep it a secret. Besides, until yesterday, I wasn't sure I'd actually get to come."

Nervously, Chelsea introduced Jillian. She wanted Lacey and Jillian to like each other. "So, you're from Texas," Lacey said, studying Jillian and then the plane off in the distance. "Is that one of your Texas-size dragonflies?"

Jillian grinned. "How'd you guess?"

"I've heard everything comes bigger in Texas. I'm glad to meet you. Chelsea's written something about you in every letter to me."

"Good stuff, I hope."

"The best."

It pleased Chelsea that Lacey was actually trying to be friendly. Chelsea had never been able to second-guess Lacey—one minute she was sweet and nice; the next, as prickly as a cactus. Katie had told her that some of Lacey's mood swings were related to her diabetes.

Chelsea listened while Lacey and Katie swapped stories about school. She felt the old, familiar twinge of envy because she'd never been able to attend a regular school. Lacey told of her fascination with Todd, and Chelsea thought of her hopeless crush on DJ.

"Just wait until Chelsea and I get our new hearts," Jillian said. "We'll have guys falling at our feet and a hundred stories to tell."

"How will we do that?" Chelsea asked. "Trip them?"

The others giggled, but Jillian waved Chelsea's comment away. "I was thinking we could use Lacey and Katie as bait, and when the guys gather like flies, we'll rope them in."

"That's what I've always dreamed of—a guy hog-tied at my feet," Chelsea remarked with a straight face.

"We'll charm them over. Who knows? New hearts may make us real daring."

The car wound its way up the drive of Jenny House. Only months before, the trees had been thick and green with leaves. Now, the last vestiges of autumn color clung to the few leaves that still hung on the branches. "Fall's pretty," Lacey commented, staring out the window. "Where I come from, it's always summertime."

"Same way in Texas," Jillian declared. "Course, if I asked Daddy, he'd paint the leaves like autumn for me." She paused, then added with a grin, "If we had trees in Texas."

They all laughed, including Mr. Holloway. The car rounded a bend, and Jenny House came into view. The great stone, glass, and wood building, surrounded by jutting wooden decks, looked as sturdy as the mountains behind it. The sight brought a lump to Chelsea's throat. What a wonderful time she'd had here last summer, in spite of losing Amanda. Jenny House had been her first real escape from her world of sickness and hospitals.

"Welcome to our little cabin in the woods," Mr. Holloway said, pulling the car as close to the front wooden deck as possible.

"Some cabin," Jillian declared. "I like it."

"Good thing," he replied. "It'd be tough to rebuild in a weekend if you didn't like it."

The staff greeted the girls, who followed Mr. Holloway up to the dorm room that had been theirs during the summer.

"I wasn't sure if you'd want your old room or not," he said. "I thought I'd let you decide."

Except for Jillian, all their gazes focused on the bed that had been Amanda's.

"This will be fine," Katie said after making eye contact with Lacey and Chelsea for their approval. "This one's yours, Jillian." Katie walked briskly to Amanda's former bed and tossed Jillian's small duffel bag beside it.

Jillian stretched out and patted the bedspread. "Baby Bear thinks this bed is just right. And she'll take real good care of it."

Katie jogged down the trail, kicking up dry leaves as she ran. She hoped Lacey was already waiting at the small rest area midway between Jenny House and the walking trail. Katie would have been on time for their meeting if she hadn't waited while the nurse had settled Jillian and Chelsea for afternoon naps. But she had waited, feeling a responsibility toward her two friends she was unable to explain.

Katie leapt over a tree branch that had fallen across the trail without breaking stride. In March, track season would begin, and with it, her final shot at a track scholarship. She needed to stay in shape. She jogged off the trail, through a stand of trees, and saw the wooden table and benches in the distance. Lacey was sitting atop the table, her hands shoved deep in the pockets of a wool jacket.

"Sorry I'm late," Katie said as she came to the table. She sat on the bench, facing toward Lacey.

"Aren't you even winded?" Lacey asked.

"It's only half a mile," Katie insisted. "The mile run is my best event, you know."

"Whoopee," Lacey grumbled through chattering teeth. "It's cold out here. When I left Miami, it was seventy-five degrees. Why couldn't we have met down in one of the rec rooms?"

"I didn't think about it," Katie admitted. "I like being outside."

"Well, back-to-nature isn't my best event." Lacey hugged her jacket tighter to herself. "Before I forget and before you think I'm an ingrate, thanks for the airplane ticket up here. I couldn't have come if you hadn't sent me the money. And I really wanted to come."

"It's no big deal," Katie said. "I dipped into my Wish money, but that's what it's there for—to do a few things I want to do when I want to do them. Besides, I got a real cheap fare."

"Anyway, it was nice of you. I was green with envy thinking about the three of you coming here without me. Jillian is quite a character, isn't she?"

"I like her. She's been great for Chelsea. I'm in school, and she's got nothing else to do but lie around the house all day and wait for her beeper to go off. I can tell you from personal experience, it's no picnic."

"She has a tutor, doesn't she?"

"Yes, but that gets boring too."

"Tell me about it. If it weren't for attending classes and studying, school would be the perfect place for me."

Katie laughed. "I like school, so I can't identify.

So far this year, I'm doing great. I've got A's and B's going in every class, especially—"

Lacey held up her hand, stopping Katie's flood of words. "Let's just cut to the bottom line, Katie, before I freeze to death out here."

"What do you mean? What bottom line?"

Lacey leaned downward until her nose was inches from Katie's. "I want to know the reason you told me to meet you. The *real* reason you bought me the ticket and wanted me to come all the way to Jenny House for three days. Tell me, Katie. I'm waiting."

Ten

FLUSTERED, KATIE GLANCED around the woods as if checking to see if anyone else might be listening. "I don't know what you mean. I wanted you to be with us. Just like this summer."

"I appreciate that. What I don't appreciate is freezing my butt off out here because you want to talk privately and can't figure a better place to meet."

Katie suppressed a smile. "Don't be cross. You're right. . . . I do want to talk to you privately."

"I knew it!" Lacey straightened triumphantly. "I knew something else was going on. So, tell me. What's up?"

Katie looked sheepish, but refused to be hurried. "First, I want you to tell me how things are for you at home. Your letters sound full of doom and gloom."

Lacey's pretty mouth formed a thin line. "Same old, same old," she said. "My parents aren't making it. I'm betting that once the Christmas holidays are over, Dad will move out."

Katie felt a sinking sensation. "That's too bad." She remembered when her own parents were having troubles, but things had cleared up once the pressure of her transplant was off. Once it was evident she was going to live. "Are you sure?"

"I'm sure. Dad's sleeping in the guest room every night. So—are you going to tell me what's going on with you or not?"

Suddenly, Katie's personal problems seemed petty and small. She shouldn't be dumping on Lacey, who obviously had *real* problems. "It's kind of dumb really," Katie began.

"Don't let that stop you."

Katie took a deep breath. "I've been having second thoughts about Josh and me."

Lacey looked stunned. "You and Josh? But, Katie, you two are like an institution. A fixture. I remember how crazy you were about each other this summer. What's gone wrong?"

"Nothing . . . really. I'm just not sure I should be so serious about him. I mean, I want to go away to college and all, and if I go far away, how can we keep together? It's not fair for us to expect each other to not date anyone else. Is it?"

Lacey's eyes narrowed. "Is there another guy in your life, Katie?"

Katie felt color creep up her neck and a hot wave of embarrassment roll over her. Was she so transparent that Lacey had seen through her so quickly? "Um—not exactly." The image of Garrison intruded into her thoughts. "There *is* a guy in my English class. We've been working on a paper together—a very important paper. It'll count for half of our semester grade. Anyway, I spend a lot of time with him because of the paper, and Josh isn't very happy about it."

She stopped her story, but the silence seemed deafening. Lacey studied her, her gaze full of speculation. "What are you leaving out, Katie? I feel as if I'm only hearing part of a play and have to figure out for myself what's going on."

"Well, the guy—his name's Garrison—is attractive to me," Katie explained almost apologetically. "But I'm having trouble deciding what he wants from me."

Lacey arched an eyebrow. "I'm certainly no authority on boys. But I know what most of them want."

Katie ignored Lacey's barb. "I remember how you handled Jeff this summer. You were in total control."

"I avoided Jeff," Lacey corrected. "I couldn't mess with him once I knew how Amanda felt about him."

"But you admitted he caused fireworks when he kissed you."

Lacey hopped down off the table and straddled the bench so that she was directly in front of Katie.

"Are you telling me you've been kissing this guy behind Josh's back?"

Katie leapt up. "Absolutely not! I never have—"

"But you would like to," Lacey finished matter-of-factly.

Katie's face flushed crimson again. Why couldn't she admit that Lacey was right? She'd wanted Garrison to kiss her more than once, but so far, he'd kept his distance. All he did was ask cryptic questions and drive wedges of doubt through her mind about her feelings for Josh.

Lacey reached up and took Katie's arm, forcing her back down onto the bench. "Why don't you start at the very beginning and tell little Lacey the whole story," she said.

Katie did. She left nothing out, including the night in the student union and the question Garrison had asked that had haunted her for weeks. *"Is it love or gratitude?"* By the time she finished her story, a wind had risen and whipped leaves around their ankles. She shivered, but Lacey, who earlier had been so cold, seemed oblivious to the wind's chill. "Now you've heard everything," Katie declared. "What do you think?"

"I think this guy is a snake. I think he's just messing with your head. Some guys like to mess with a girl's brain. They like the feeling of being in control. Of having power. What *you're* feeling toward him is only hormones."

Katie gritted her teeth. She'd poured out her confused emotions, and Lacey had reduced it all to body chemistry. She'd hoped for a more illuminating appraisal. "Thanks a lot," she replied un-kindly. "I could have gotten that much if I'd told my mother!"

"What do you want to hear? That it's all right for you to dump Josh and go hot and heavy into a thing with this guy? I won't tell you that, Katie. Josh and you have a history. He's been there for you through good and bad. You were nuts about him, and not just because of his brother's heart. You told us how he helped you train for those Transplant Games and how he gave you the locket you wear."

Self-consciously, Katie fingered the gold heart and chain that lay in the hollow of her throat be-neath her thick turtleneck sweater, and recalled the night Josh had given it to her. He'd kissed her tenderly. Now, her heart thumped uncontrollably when Garrison was close to her too. Whenever he looked at her with his soul-melting brown eyes. Maybe Lacey was right. Maybe it was only hor-mones.

Katie buried her face in her hands. "I'm all mixed up, Lacey. I don't know what I'm feeling. I don't think I can even trust my feelings anymore."

Lacey put her arm around Katie's shoulders. "I don't like giving advice, Katie. I don't take it very well either, come to think of it."

Katie smiled in spite of herself. "I didn't want you engineering that 'romance' between Jeff and Amanda this summer, but in the end, things turned out all right."

"Maybe so in that particular case. However, no

one can decide what's the right thing to do in your case except *you*. Breaking it off with Josh would hurt a lot. But so would sticking around if you're not right for each other. I've always believed in playing the field."

"But you refuse to play around with Jeff," Katie observed dryly.

Lacey dropped her arm and backed away. "That's different. You know my reasons for avoiding Jeff. As for you, you may need to have a fling with this Garrison in order to decide what's best for you. Just don't do it behind Josh's back."

"I wouldn't." Katie chewed her lower lip nervously. "It's such a big decision. I don't want to hurt Josh. I really do love him."

Lacey offered a wry smile. "Love is a four-letter word, Katie. Be careful how you toss it around."

Katie nodded and returned Lacey's smile. "Come on—let's go back. It's getting late, and it's getting colder. Your lips are starting to look as blue as Chelsea's and Jillian's."

Lacey made a face and joined Katie on the trail, where together they walked back to the warmth and light of Jenny House.

After breakfast Saturday morning, Chelsea took Jillian down to the rec room at Jenny House. A number of other kids were already there, kids Chelsea didn't know from the summer, but who were obviously enjoying the unique environment. She saw that the staff had added another virtual reality game, one that enclosed up to two players in a cocoonlike bubble lined with video screens so that the players were surrounded.

She chose a program and sat on the double-size chair with Jillian and in minutes became absorbed in a fantasy featuring downhill skiing. The experience was so encompassing, so totally immersing, that during one sequence of having to leap a precarious chasm, Chelsea felt Jillian grab her arm and heard her gasp.

"That was something else," Jillian said. "Totally real. I've always wanted to ski, but of course, I never could."

"VR is the next-best thing," Chelsea said. "All the fun and none of the risks."

Jillian tipped her head and looked thoughtful. "That's true, but I like knowing there're risks. Risks are what make life fun."

They left the game room and took the elevator up to the main floor. They sat on the long sofa in front of the fireplace. Logs burned in the great hearth, taking the November chill from the air. "Why take risks if you don't have to?" Chelsea asked.

"Because risks make a person feel excited and alive."

"The game makes me feel excited." Chelsea defended her choice of VR over real life. "It seems to me that taking risks can also mean losing out on something. At least in VR, you know you're safe."

Jillian waved off Chelsea's comment. "Who wants to be safe? Don't you like living on the edge?"

"The edge of what? Death? No, thanks. . . . I've lived there all my life. All I want now is a nice, safe life."

Jillian shook her head. "Life should be an adventure. Once I get my transplant, I may go save the rain forests. Do you ever think about doing something grand with your life, Chelsea? I mean, if I hadn't been born sick, what would I have done with myself? Would I spend time volunteering in a hospital, helping people? Or would I have been like Shelby, thinking about no one but myself? Sometimes, people who are born perfect, who never have to hurt or want for anything, seem stunted."

"Life's not an adventure to me, Jillian. It's a scary place full of pain. I've never told a living soul this, but I'm more afraid of getting that transplant than of not getting it. So afraid that I'm not even sure I want to go through with it."

Eleven

"**N**OT GO THROUGH with it? You can't be serious!"

The shocked expression on Jillian's face made Chelsea wish she'd kept her thoughts to herself. "Well, maybe just a part of me is scared of going through with it."

"You'd want to spend the rest of your life gasping for air and passing out when your heart goes haywire? Not me. I can't wait for the transplant."

"But what if . . . what if I die during the operation?" There. Chelsea had voiced her darkest fear.

"But we'll die without the operation," Jillian replied matter-of-factly. "When they did surgery on me before, I thought they were going to fix me once and for all. When I found out that not much had changed, I cried for days. So far as I'm concerned, I'd rather be dead than an invalid the rest of my life."

"I wish I wasn't so scared. I wish I was brave like you and Katie."

Jillian wrinkled her nose self-consciously. "I'm not brave. I just don't want to compromise. Besides, if I die, I hope to go to heaven, where I'll be given a perfect body, as well as straight hair and no freckles." She grinned. "So I figure, either way, I win."

Chelsea felt ashamed that she didn't have faith or hope like Jillian's.

"If I don't get well, DJ will kill me."

"Why?"

"Because he's my older brother, and he says he's supposed to go first."

"But you're twins."

"He was born three minutes ahead of me, so that makes me the baby."

Now it was Chelsea who smiled. "Some baby."

"You're the only one I'd say this to," Jillian said soberly, "but I worry about DJ."

"Whatever for? He's healthy . . . isn't he?"

"He's healthy. But he's not real strong inside the way I am."

"I don't know what you mean."

"I'm not sure I can explain it." Jillian toyed with a sofa cushion as she talked. "When we were little, when I'd get sick, he'd stand next to my bed and cry. I can remember how he would hold on to my hand and beg me to get well. Like I had a choice. But sometimes, when I'm really having a hard time, I can still hear his voice begging me. Sometimes, it's all I have to keep me going. He feels guilty, and I know it's not his fault. It's nobody's fault really."

"You're lucky to have him," Chelsea said. "I've wished for a bigger family. Good thing Katie and Lacey became like sisters to me."

"Can I be your sister too?"

"You already are."

Jillian's expression grew mischievous. "But you don't want DJ for a brother. I mean, with you having a crush on him, it wouldn't be proper."

"Don't tease me about DJ. Nothing will ever come of it anyway."

"We'll see."

Chelsea gave her a sideways glance. "You better not do anything to embarrass me with him."

"Me?" Jillian flapped her eyelashes innocently. "I wouldn't dream of such a thing."

Chelsea didn't believe her, but didn't want to push the issue.

"I guess she did good things with her money, didn't she?" Jillian pointed up at the portrait of Jenny.

"She did. But not all of us have money. We don't have anything to give away that's important."

"Not true," Jillian replied with a toss of her wild mass of red hair. "Take you, for instance. You have yourself. I figure that's the nicest present of all, Chelsea James being herself—being my best friend."

With Jillian's comment, goose bumps spread over Chelsea. The rich girl with the Texas-size heart really liked her. Her friendship with Katie, Lacey, and Amanda had been born of mutual suffering and proximity during the summer. But with Jillian, although they had similar medical problems, Chelsea felt that they would have been friends sick or well. Near or far. Perhaps that's what Jenny Crawford had meant when she'd signed Katie's Wish Letter *Your Forever Friend.*

A friend was someone who liked you—fears and all.

It was early Saturday afternoon before Chelsea could wangle time alone with Lacey. The private-duty nurse had insisted that Jillian nap, and Katie had taken off on one of her long runs. Lacey was heading down to the game room when Chelsea called her over to the sofa in front of the fireplace. "Sit down a minute and talk to me. I've been wanting to ask you some things."

Lacey joined her on the couch, curled her long legs beneath her, and snuggled into the cushions. "I didn't mean to ignore you. When's that fancy jet of Jillian's heading out?"

"Tomorrow after lunch. How about you?"

"A staffer is taking me to the airport early in the morning. My plane leaves at nine."

"Then all we have is the rest of today and tonight," Chelsea said with a sigh. "Boy, I hate leaving this place."

"Me too, in a way. But lots is going on back home."

"It didn't sound like things are great for you, but you sure sound busy."

"There's no such thing as too busy for me."

Chelsea took a deep breath. "How's your diabetes doing? You know—your blood sugar control?" She knew enough from the summer to understand that the tighter control Lacey kept on her blood sugar levels, the better she would feel and function day to day.

"You're not my doctor," Lacey grumbled. "Honestly, you and Katie both act as if I don't have good sense. I'm taking care of myself."

There was something in Lacey's defensive tone that made Chelsea doubt her. "Oh, really? You look to me like you've lost weight."

"Who wants to be fat?"

"You're not fat."

Lacey made a face. "Mirrors don't lie. Most of the girls in my crowd are thin as pencils. They look so cool and wear the neatest clothes. Sizes five or seven. I'm still a size eleven and feel like a cow next to them. Besides, Mom's so busy with work and fighting with Dad, she hardly ever cooks anymore."

"Can't you cook?"

"Oh, please!" Lacey rolled her eyes dramatically. "I hate the kitchen."

"But it seems to me like you should know how to cook the right foods—"

"Stop," Lacey interrupted. "You sound like a dietitian. I don't need this from you."

"All right, forget the health lecture. How's Todd Larson?"

Lacey shrugged and glanced toward the logs crackling in the hearth. "He's the coolest guy in the high school, and he can have his pick of any girl he wants. He's rich and drives a bright red Miata, and he's paid some attention to me. But every girl's after him."

"Does he know about your diabetes?"

"Get real. Why would I tell a guy about *that*?"

"In case you had an insulin reaction on a date." Chelsea thought her answer was perfectly logical, but Lacey reacted to it instantly.

"Why would I make an issue of a turnoff like a disease. Guys aren't interested in girls with problems."

"Jeff was."

"Don't you start in on me," Lacey snapped. "Katie's already told me what a mistake I made in letting Jeff get away. As far as I'm concerned, Jeff is ancient history, and I have no plans to excavate the past." She stood up, which was Lacey's way of saying the conversation was over. "Let's not ruin things here. Come downstairs with me and we'll play a game of VR."

Chelsea was tempted, but she had another idea and knew that if she was going to manage it, she'd need to rest. "Actually, I'd like you and Katie to do something with me later. Maybe before supper tonight."

"What?"

Chelsea rubbed her temples, fighting off fatigue. "More than anything, I want to take Jillian up to the mountain Amanda took us to. The one where we put her memorial sign. Will you get the horses ready and go with us?"

Twelve

THE FOURSOME HAD to leave Jenny House by three-thirty in order to get up the mountain and back down again before dark. Jillian's private-duty nurse was against the trip, but Jillian argued persuasively to get her way. Jillian won. "If we're not back by five, send out a posse," she called to the anxious-looking nurse as the trail horses left the stables and headed into the North Carolina woods.

Chelsea had the same horse she'd ridden during the summer. He was lazy, but she felt safe on him. She looked down as she rode, watching his hooves strike the packed brown, dead leaves. Above, bare tree branches soared into a cloudy gray sky. The air felt raw and cold, not like the humid weather of July. She shivered and pulled the sheepskin jacket she'd borrowed from Jillian tighter around her.

Earlier, when she'd first mentioned the ride to Lacey, her friend hadn't been enthusiastic. "I'm not sure I want to share the place with anybody else," Lacey had said pointedly. "It was Mandy's. And ours."

"But Jillian's one of us," Chelsea countered.

"She hasn't got a history with us."

Chelsea hated it when Lacey grew stubborn. "Listen, history for Jillian and me might be brief."

Lacey waved aside Chelsea's pessimism. "We promised Amanda it would be our place alone. Don't you remember?"

"She'd be the first to want us to share it," Chelsea insisted. "I know she wouldn't want to hold us to that promise."

"We made plans with one another to meet up there this summer. It's only fall. If you keep your promise, and get *better*"—she stabbed her finger into Chelsea's chest—"let Jillian come with us then."

"You know I will if I can, but we're at Jenny House *now*, and I want to take Jillian up the mountain *now*."

Just then, Katie entered the lobby, breathing hard from her run, her hooded sweatshirt damp with perspiration. Chelsea called her over and explained her plan.

"I think it's a good idea," Katie said after a minute of thought. "I've wanted to go and check out the memorial myself, but wasn't sure if the two of you wanted to go."

"I want to go," Lacey replied. "I'm just not sure about taking Jillian."

"Then *we'll* take her," Kate said. "And you can go whenever you like."

Chelsea admired the firm way Katie handled Lacey without being rude or argumentative.

"Oh, all right," Lacey grumbled once she realized Katie wouldn't back down. "Do you think we can pry her away from her nurse, or are we going to have to take the entire staff and Mr. Holloway with us?"

"Leave the nurse to Jillian," Chelsea said with an exasperated smile over Lacey's sarcasm. "She'll shed her one way or another."

Now, as they plodded up the looping trail, Chelsea felt herself growing apprehensive. The sight of the memorial and the memories it evoked might be too sad. What if they all started crying? What would Jillian think?

"This way!" Katie called. A small piece of faded yellow material Amanda had tied to a tree marked the ascent up the mountainside.

Jillian brought her horse alongside Chelsea's. "Boy, does it feel good to be riding again."

The effortless way Jillian rode, as if she were one with the horse, impressed Chelsea. "You ride like a cowgirl," she said. "I never rode until this summer, and my fanny hurt for three days."

Jillian laughed. "Daddy had me sitting on a

horse from the time I was a baby. Even though I was sick, he bought me my first pony when I was three. DJ had a matching one, and the two of us learned to ride together. Of course, DJ got better at it because he did it more often. When we were ten, we got quarter horses—mine is a roan. I named him Windsong. DJ has a chestnut he calls Cochise. He rides him in rodeo competitions, and no one can chase down a calf and tie it down faster than DJ."

She sighed, and some of the sparkle left her eyes. "That's something else I want to do when I get a new heart. I want to ride in the rodeo."

Chelsea couldn't imagine such a thing. Plodding along on a horse as tame as the ones at Jenny House was about as much adventure as she could handle. "I hope you get to do it."

"When we both get these operations behind us, you can come out to our ranch in the summer. I'll teach you how to ride and rope and cut cattle."

"Are those marketable skills?" Chelsea asked with a laugh. "I always thought I'd like to be a teacher. Or a guide and lecturer in a museum of art."

"Why would you want to be around people all day? Give me the wide open spaces anytime."

"I guess because I've never been around people. I've been stuck off by myself most of my life. I get lonely."

Jillian shook her head. "Don't you know you can sometimes be lonely even in a crowd of people?"

"Are you? The way your family rallies around you, it's hard to believe."

"Sometimes. Maybe it's because of my medical history. Hospitals have a way of making a person feel less than a person."

Chelsea knew that much was true. Some of her hospitalizations had been positively dehumanizing. "Sometimes they treat you as if you were a machine with a bad gear."

Chelsea laughed as Jillian told her a story.

"What's so funny?" Lacey called over her shoulder.

"Just hospital stories," Chelsea replied, wiping the sleeve of her coat across her eyes, which teared with her laughter.

"*Nothing's* funny about hospitals," Lacey insisted.

Up ahead, Katie had stopped and tied her horse's reins to a tree. When the others arrived, Katie said, "We'll have to go the rest of the way on foot."

Chelsea looked to Jillian, who seemed to be breathing harder.

"Thin air," Jillian explained, dismounting. "But I can make it."

By the time Chelsea had walked her up to the crest of the plateau, Katie and Lacey were crouching and cleaning off an accumulation of leaves from the ground. Chelsea felt her heart pounding from exertion, so she led Jillian to a jutting boulder and sat down next to her. Beneath her lipstick, Jillian's lips appeared quite blue. Chelsea felt a momentary stab of fear. She fervently hoped they hadn't presumed too much about Jillian's strength.

"Here's the top of the cross," Lacey called out excitedly.

Chelsea watched as the leaves were strewn aside and a cross of rocks emerged. "Lacey constructed it with her own hands in tribute to Amanda," Chelsea told Jillian.

"And here're the sticks," Katie called, picking up a tripod of wood and standing it upright. "It's still intact."

"Let us see."

Carefully, Katie and Lacey carried the makeshift memorial over to where Chelsea and Jillian were sitting. "When it stands upright, it forms a tepee," Chelsea explained.

Katie sat it down, and a photo dangled precariously from a string. Jillian leaned forward and picked up a corner of the photo, now faded and dirtied by the weather. "That's the four of us in front of the fireplace at Jenny House," Chelsea continued. "That's Mandy in the middle."

Jillian said, "She's cute. And what a smile."

Chelsea felt a lump swell inside her throat. Amanda looked so happy. Only months before, she'd been alive. And breathing. Chelsea shivered anew and tugged the coat against her. "She was a doll all right."

"She discovered this place," Lacey said, pointing. "We came up here after a rainstorm and built this for her."

Traces of the lipstick heart Katie had drawn on the photo could barely be seen.

"It was a beautiful summer day, there was a rainbow, and it seemed as if she was right here with us." Katie's voice sounded thick with emotion.

"I can retie the photo," Jillian offered. She pulled a fringe of leather from the suede jacket beneath her heavier coat. "This will last longer than the string," she said. "The Indians used leather to tie things together all the time."

Chelsea watched through a film of tears as Jillian's fingers knotted the piece of leather through the hole where the string was rotting away. "There," Jillian said, holding it up. "How's that?"

"Looks good," Katie whispered.

"Amanda told us that at night, elves and fairies came and danced in the moonlight. So I'm going to set the tripod up again at the head of the cross. That way she can watch them when they come."

Lacey reached for the tepee, but Jillian pulled it back. "Wait," she said. "I'd like to leave a little gift for Amanda too." Jillian pulled off her gloves and unfastened a diamond stud earring from her right ear. With effort, she pushed the sharp end of the stud through the photo directly above Amanda's head. Even in the failing gray light, the diamond gleamed.

"You're leaving a real diamond out *here?*" Lacey asked, wide-eyed.

"I figure that a fairy queen should have a real

crown," Jillian replied. Her freckled skin looked pale, and her eyes large and luminous.

Chelsea felt a tear slide down her cheek. "Thank you, Jillian," she whispered.

Katie squeezed Jillian's hands. "Put your gloves on," she said. "You're cold as ice."

"We made a pact to come back this summer," Lacey blurted.

"Are you inviting me?" Jillian asked.

"It wouldn't be the same coming without you," Lacey told her. "But you've got to promise to show up," she added emphatically. "That's the only rule. You've got to promise."

"I will if I can," Jillian said solemnly.

"We should start back down." Katie stood.

They walked, arm in arm, toward the horses. Chelsea glanced backward once. She saw where Lacey had reanchored the tripod at the head of the stone cross. A cold breeze lifted the photo and sent it fluttering. The diamond caught the light and tossed off a tiny spark, like a shimmering beacon . . . only for the eyes of elves and fairies.

Thirteen

"I DON'T KNOW WHY you're dragging us to this party, Katie. I'd rather be alone with you tonight." Josh turned off his car engine in front of the brightly lit house in one of Ann Arbor's better residential sections.

"I told you why. Garrison invited us—both of us—and since we've finished our English project and today was the last day of classes and, therefore, the start of Christmas break, I *feel* like going to his party. It won't kill you to hang around for a few hours." Katie struggled to keep her voice light, but deep down, she was seething. Why was Josh being such a pain about attending Garrison's party? Didn't he realize how tense her life was these days?

Soon after returning from Jenny House, Chelsea

had taken a downward turn. She was bedridden at Katie's house, and needed oxygen almost around the clock. It hadn't been so long that Katie had forgotten what it was like to be tethered to an oxygen tank. She shivered, although Josh's car was still warm from the heater.

"Well, if you're determined to go to this thing," Josh grumbled, "then let's get it over with." He stormed out of the car.

Katie opened her door and brushed past him. "Don't do me any favors."

"Hey, wait up."

Katie didn't pause, but hurried up the walkway in the biting night air.

In spite of the cold, kids congregated on the front porch, and from inside, stereo speakers blared with the latest rock music. Katie pushed inside the front door and encountered another swarm of kids. Secretly, she wasn't too keen on attending the party either, but she knew she couldn't back out now. She wedged her way past several dancing couples into a large, beautifully decorated living room. More kids sat on pillowed sofas and in oversize chairs and on the floor near a giant Christmas tree dressed with Victorian-style ornaments.

"Katie!" Garrison called her name, and she turned to see him make his way through a group of seniors. "I'm glad you came. I wasn't sure you would when I invited you." He wore a heart-melting smile.

"Is there anybody from school you *didn't* invite?" she asked.

He laughed. "Here's what happened. I invited a few people to a party, and they invited a few, who invited a few, and so on. It's like growing a fungus in a petri dish. Take your coat?" He brushed her shoulders.

She took a step away, hesitant to have him touch her. "How will you ever find it again when I want to leave?"

"Don't worry. I will." His brown eyes bore into her until she felt self-conscious. "Where's Josh? Did he come with you?"

Just then Josh elbowed his way alongside Katie. "I got you a soda," he said, handing Katie a cup and eyeing Garrison.

She sipped the drink because her throat suddenly felt tight and parched. "Nice tree," she remarked, nodding toward the Christmas tree.

"My mother's a collector of special ornaments."

"Where are your parents?" Josh asked the question.

"They left hours ago. They hate loud noise and anything but classical music." He flashed his charming smile. "Just so long as the cops don't have to come, we'll be all right."

Remembering how easy he was to talk to, how clever he was with words, Katie returned his smile. She felt Josh take her hand possessively. "Let's dance."

"Is that an invitation or a command?" She was fed up with Josh's behavior.

Josh scowled. His eyes looked angry, and she felt tension in his grip. "I didn't know I needed to beg a dance with my girl."

Garrison backed away. "Look, I should mingle. If you want to talk later . . ."

The invitation was open-ended and to both of them, but Katie knew how Josh would take it. As soon as Garrison was out of earshot, she snatched her hand from Josh's. "You humiliated me in front of him on purpose."

"You were all but throwing yourself at him."

"That's not true!" By now, Katie was so angry, she was shaking. "What's wrong with you? Why are you acting like a jealous idiot? I hate it, Josh."

"Me? Jealous of that jerk? Get real! You're the one flirting with him."

"You listen to me, Josh Martel. I've had ample opportunity to flirt with him, and I never have!"

"Give me a break. I've seen the way you two look at each other. A blind man could see it."

Katie's jaw went slack. She couldn't believe Josh was saying these things to her. Hurting her with words that hit like stones. "Well, if you've got twenty-twenty vision," she hissed, "watch this!" Katie turned and walked away as quickly as she could forge a path through the crowds. Hot tears stung her eyes, and her chin trembled. She shoved her way along until she was at the top of the basement stairs. Quickly, she descended to where softer music played and couples danced by candlelight, entwined around one another.

A survey of the room told her that she was the

only single person in it. She spun to return to the noisier party above and ran smack into Garrison's chest. "Trouble in paradise?" he asked.

Tears threatened, but she didn't like Garrison's attitude either. "There's nothing wrong between me and Josh."

"You could have fooled me." He smoothed her hair. "Calm down, Katie."

"I should have Josh take me home," she said quietly, self-conscious under his gaze.

"Why? You're here now, and if I'm not mistaken, your ride's gone off and left you."

"Josh left?" He'd abandoned her!

"I'll take you home."

"But it's *your* party."

"Exactly. I can do whatever I want. But first, come sit with me for a minute." He led her over to a bar, its top heaped with sodas, chips, and empty cups, and sat her down on a high stool. He stood directly in front of her and lifted her chin with his forefinger. "This fight with Josh is my fault, isn't it?"

"It's his fault," she declared. "He's making up things and letting his imagination go crazy."

"He just cares about you. If you were my girl, I might act the same way."

If you were my girl . . . She refused to look Garrison in the eye, unsure of what to say. If only she could think of something funny. Lacey's words came back to her. *"He's just messing with your head."* Was it true? Was Garrison merely playing some elaborate game with her? "Maybe you're right. I am his girlfriend, and I made him bring me tonight."

"I *was* surprised to see you."

"Can you take me home now?"

He put his hand on her arm. "Why rush off? You're here—have some fun."

She glanced at the dancing couples, heard the soft, romantic music spilling through the air, watched the flickering candlelight. "I feel out of place."

"Would you like to dance?"

"No." The word was out before she even had a chance to think about it.

"There's no crime in dancing with me. You and Josh aren't engaged."

His logic was cool and on target, and Katie realized that she did want to dance with him. She wanted to experience being in his arms, satisfy her curiosity once and for all. "I don't think so," she heard herself saying.

Garrison gave her a long, searching look. "Your loyalty is commendable." His smile flashed. "And frustrating."

She shrugged sheepishly. "It just wouldn't be right. Not to me, anyway."

From across the room, one of Garrison's friends called, "Hey, Garrison, quit talking and look up."

Simultaneously, Katie and Garrison looked. Above them, a sprig of mistletoe dangled from a string someone had thumbtacked to the ceiling. It fluttered slightly from the heated air circulating in the room.

"Looks like a perfect opportunity to me," Garrison said.

Katie watched his mouth descend. She wanted to push away, wanted to duck and run, but she felt caught. And like a moth lured by a flame, she felt her chin lift toward him in slow, irresistible increments.

Garrison's lips held hers for a sweet, delicious minute that sent her blood racing and her heart singing. Yet even before the kiss was over, she felt the unmistakable dagger of guilt pierce through her. Not only because she knew she was betraying Josh, but because she enjoyed Garrison's lingering kiss to the depths of her soul.

Chelsea woke, gasping for air. Cold sweat soaked through the sheets of her bed, and pain squeezed her chest like an iron vise. She struggled for air, sucked greedily from the oxygen mask over her face, but the pure oxygen supplement brought no relief. The pain radiated in heated waves, shooting through her left breast and down her arm like the bite of a viper.

Chelsea tried to scream, but no sound came out. She tried to move, but felt pinned to her mattress like a butterfly trapped under glass, unable to flutter its wings. The pain intensified. Her heart raced, thudded, and sputtered. Its rhythm felt out of sync, as if it might tumble out of its cavity and spill out of her body.

Pinwheels of light burst behind her eyeballs, and an ominous edge of blackness crept over her mind, storm clouds blotting out the light. *"Help me!"* her brain cried. Her hand groped for the bed-side table, shoved over the clock, knocked a book to the floor, then miraculously closed around the bell Katie had given her.

She believed she actually heard it ringing before the darkness descended and enveloped her in its cold arms.

Fourteen

KATIE STARED THROUGH the glass partition of Cardiac ICU, feeling numb and icy cold. Chelsea lay unconscious on the bed while all around her, machines hummed and beeped. Mindless machines that held Chelsea's fragile life signs within their mechanical grip.

The cardiac monitor sent a ragged line over its view scope, reminding Katie of fishing line tossed at random and snagged by the wind. The line dipped, then skipped. Its monotonous beeping tone pulsated inside Katie's brain and left her trembling. She didn't have to be a cardiologist to realize that her friend was dying.

When her ten minutes were up, Katie returned to the small waiting room where her parents sat with Chelsea's parents. Chelsea's mother had found her daughter unconscious after being awakened by the ringing of Chelsea's bedside bell. Somehow, in the midst of her pain, Chelsea had managed to get hold of it. Katie shuddered, thinking what could have happened if she hadn't gotten hold of the bell.

Her doctor had told them down in ER that Chelsea had succumbed to a heart attack. Her poor old heart was simply worn out. She needed the transplant. Except that she'd been waiting for months, and no donor had been found. And now, her situation appeared desperate. But medical science was full of tricks. Perhaps it held one more for Chelsea.

Katie shook her head to clear it. Her brain was so tired of going over and over the same old territory. She told herself she should make some calls. Lacey should know what was happening. And Jillian. The clock on the wall said five A.M. Katie couldn't call anyone just yet. Why alarm friends until she had more to tell them?

Dr. Dawson, Chelsea's physician at the medical center, swept into the room, and instantly, everyone rose. He clasped Chelsea's parents' hands. "She's stable," he told them. "And she's holding her own."

"Thank God," Mrs. James sobbed.

Katie felt her knees go weak. While Chelsea wasn't out of the woods yet, she was better off than Katie had thought. Stability meant that her heart was pumping, and as long as it continued to pump, Chelsea was alive.

"I have other news," Dr. Dawson said. "We received a call about an hour ago that there's a *possibility*"—he emphasized the word—"a fair possibility that we have a donor heart available."

With his words, Katie's gaze flew upward. She heard Chelsea's parents ask, "Who? When will you know for sure? Is Chelsea strong enough to withstand the surgery?"

Dr. Dawson patted Chelsea's mother's hand. "The victim is a seventeen-year-old girl in Columbus, Ohio. Her snowmobile hit a tree, and she sustained a massive head injury. She's on life support now, but she's about to be declared brain dead. The blood type is compatible, and so are her weight and size. Her family has agreed to her being a donor."

Katie felt a mix of jumbled emotions. She recoiled at hearing the girl was being kept alive by machines, yet she experienced wild hope for Chelsea's sake.

The doctor continued. "Our transplant team has been notified, and they're coming in. A surgeon has been dispatched by helicopter and jet to the hospital in Columbus, and if the heart looks good, he'll remove it, pack it in a container of dry ice, and bring it back here. It can hold up for approximately four hours this way."

Katie saw Mrs. James shiver. She felt a wave of nausea herself. Someone's heart—a stranger's—would be cut out and whisked away to save someone else's life. The process seemed both miraculous and macabre. Involuntarily, her hand slipped to her chest, where she felt the steady beat of her own transplanted heart. Aaron's heart.

Dr. Dawson said, "This girl's parents are donating all their daughter's organs, so many lives will be affected by their gift."

"Will Chelsea get her heart?" Mr. James wanted to know.

"That's not positive," Dr. Dawson said, making Katie's hopes plummet.

"But you said her blood type and body size were compatible," Mrs. James replied. Her voice sounded desperate, and Katie's mother put her arm around the woman's shoulders.

"That's true. But our philosophy is, 'Do all that can be done medically for each patient.' Chelsea's not our only patient in need. Medications are helping her now, and that may move her away from the immediate need for a transplant."

"But that's terrible!" Mrs. James cried. "She needs the transplant, and it's taken so long to find a donor. She may not survive the next heart attack. You may not be able to pull her back, and then she'll die. She'll die!" She buried her face in her hands.

Chelsea's father attempted to console her. "Everything possible is being done for Chelsea," Dr. Dawson assured them sympathetically. "These aren't easy calls for us. There're so many patients awaiting donors and so few donors to go around. Hard decisions have to be made."

Katie heard what had been left unsaid. He was trying to tell them that it wasn't easy playing God.

That doctors were faced with impossible choices, life-and-death decisions where someone always lost out. It struck her then how very lucky she'd been to have gotten her heart when she did. And it dawned on her that because she'd received it when she did, someone, somewhere else had *not* gotten it—and, more than likely, had died waiting for a heart that never came.

Once the doctor had gone, Mrs. James collapsed, weeping, in her husband's arms. Katie's parents were attempting to comfort her. Katie glanced back up at the clock and was surprised to see that only forty-five minutes had passed. It had seemed like an eternity.

Suddenly, she knew she had to have someone with her who understood. Who cared. Quickly, Katie went to the phone booth on the other side of the room. There was only one person to call. There was only Josh.

"Are you okay?" These were the first words out of Josh's mouth when he swept into the waiting room less than twenty minutes later.

"I'm all right." Katie wrapped her arms around him and buried her face against his chest. "You must have set a land speed record getting here."

"I did run two red lights, but when you called, I couldn't think about anything except getting here. How's Chelsea?"

Katie told Josh all that the doctor had said. "I can't believe this is happening," she added at the conclusion of her story. "Josh, Christmas is ten days away. Chelsea can't die before Christmas." She started crying.

Josh held her and rocked her gently. "You can't let yourself think that way. They've got her stable, and maybe the donor situation will work out."

"But what if she dies during the surgery? No one can predict how that sort of thing will go."

"They couldn't predict it with you either, but you pulled through."

"But I was stronger than Chelsea in lots of ways."

"She'll be all right."

Katie sniffed and pulled away. "First Amanda. Now Chelsea. How can I lose another friend, Josh? It's not fair."

He took her hand. "Come on down to the cafeteria. I'll buy you some breakfast."

"I can't leave."

"There's nothing you can do here. And nothing's going to happen until the donor organs arrive. Come on. Some breakfast will make you feel better. And it'll give you strength for the rest of the morning."

Her parents agreed, so she allowed Josh to lead her to the elevator. Her knees felt wobbly, and she had to lean on Josh while they waited. "I'm glad you called," he said, stroking her hair. "I . . . um . . . wasn't sure if you were still speaking to me."

"I guess what happened at Garrison's is something we need to work out."

"I'm really sorry about the way I acted at that

party, Katie. And going off and leaving you was totally stupid. I was a real butthead."

Garrison's party seemed like a million years ago to Katie. As if it had happened in another lifetime. Yet, she could still recall Garrison's mouth on hers and the way her heart had pounded when he'd kissed her. Guiltily, Katie dipped her head. "I don't want to talk about that now."

"How did you get home?"

"Garrison drove me." She braced herself for Josh's jealous reaction, but it never came.

"Do you forgive me?" he asked.

His plea touched her. She knew that really, she should be the one asking forgiveness. "I wasn't very nice to you either. I knew you didn't want to go to the party, but I made you."

"I'd do anything for you, Katie. I love you."

His words stabbed at her conscience. "I love you too."

For the first time, Josh smiled. "I'm glad you called me this morning. So glad you wanted me to be here with you."

"There isn't anyone else I'd rather be with right now." *At least that much is true*, Katie told herself. She'd have to sort out the rest of her feelings later.

The elevator doors opened into the lobby area. Because it was still so early, the usually busy lobby was almost empty. The lights were still dimmed, and some of the night crew were cleaning. She noticed a wheelchair being pushed across the polished lobby floor. Katie sucked in her breath. "Jillian?" she called, hurrying over. "Is that you?"

Jillian looked up. She was holding a portable oxygen tank in her lap, and the mask was clasped to her face. An orderly pushed the wheelchair, and Mrs. Longado walked briskly beside her daughter, an anxious expression on her face. "Katie?" Jillian asked. "What are you doing here?"

"I'm here because of Chelsea," Katie replied. Josh edged alongside her.

"Is something wrong with Chelsea?" Jillian's breath came in small gasps.

"You shouldn't exert yourself," Mrs. Longado warned.

"Haven't you come to see Chelsea?" Katie asked.

"No," Jillian said, her voice a hoarse whisper. "I was beeped this morning. The doctors may have a donor for me."

Fifteen

~~~

"A DONOR?" KATIE ASKED. She suddenly noticed the plastic banded bracelet from the admitting office on Jillian's thin wrist.

"That's what the page told Mom when we were called. We called Daddy in Texas right away, and he and DJ are on their way here."

Jillian's mother intervened. "We're taking Jillian upstairs. They must run some tests at once."

"Mama, it's all right," Jillian interrupted. "We can take a minute to talk to Katie." She looked up at Katie. "What's wrong with Chelsea?"

"She had a heart attack in the middle of the night. They've got her upstairs in Cardiac Intensive Care, and she's doing better now." Katie added the last quickly when she saw the look of alarm spread over Jillian's face.

"Will she be all right?"

"Josh and I are betting she will," Katie said with a bravado she didn't feel.

"Mom, will you go see her as soon as I get settled?"

"I should be with you. Katie can keep us informed." Mrs. Longado looked hopefully at Katie.

"Of course I will."

"But she's my best friend in the whole wide world."

"I'll handle it," Katie insisted.

The orderly cleared his throat impatiently. Jillian reached out with her free hand and grasped Katie's arm. "Come see me soon as you can. And if Chelsea's awake, tell her this may be the big day I get a new heart and lungs. Tell her that she'd better get well so she can visit me while I'm recovering."

Katie nodded and watched as Jillian and her mother disappeared into the elevator.

"Katie? Honey?" Josh's voice penetrated the fog in her brain. "What's wrong? You're white as a sheet."

Katie turned to him, so sick to her stomach, she could barely form words. "Josh, Jillian's been beeped for a transplant."

"I heard. Aren't you happy for her?"

"But Josh, Chelsea needs one too."

"I know." He wore a puzzled expression as he waited for Katie to make her point.

"Don't you see? There's one donor coming in.

Only one. Who will the doctors save? Who will get the transplant?"

For a moment, Josh stared blankly as her question sank in. "Katie, you don't know for sure there's only one donor."

"Yes, I do. There's only one. One heart. Two lungs. The doctor said that the donor's family had given permission for all her organs to be donated." Katie's voice had risen with the tide of panic rising in her. "There're two people in need and only one heart."

As the truth of what Katie was saying spread over Josh, emotion crossed his face. "Do you think that's really the case? Do you think they'd have two recipients stand by when they know only one can get the organ?"

Katie felt anger rising in her. "That's exactly what it sounds like they're doing. They can't do it! It's wrong to get someone's hopes up, then dash them to bits. I want to go back upstairs and talk to the doctor," Katie insisted. "I want to know— really know—how they decide who lives and who dies."

"But—" Josh called after her.

"I can't think about anything but talking to the doctor." Katie punched the elevator button impatiently and bounded inside the instant the doors opened. Josh rode with her up to the cardiac care floor. When the doors opened, she shot out into the hall. Dr. Dawson was standing at one of the nurses' stations, writing on a chart. Katie jogged up to him and touched his shoulder. "I want to talk to you," she said.

Looking surprised, Dr. Dawson folded the chart and put it atop the desk. "What is it, Katie?" He knew her, not only because of her involvement with Chelsea, but because she was one of the transplant center's success stories.

"This donor heart that's coming—who's going to get it?"

He blinked at her, as if he didn't quite understand her question. "You heard what I told Chelsea's family. We're not sure if it will be Chelsea or not. Why are you asking?"

"Because I saw Jillian Longado in the lobby, and she said she'd been beeped. That must mean that she's a candidate for the heart too. How can you do such a thing? How can you make two people compete for the same heart?" Katie was mad; her blood was racing, and her adrenaline pumped as if she'd just run a five-minute mile.

"Katie, I don't know who's been notified about the possibility of transplantation. It's all done by computer, and when the compatibility factors coincide, patients are notified."

"But they can't *all* get transplants," she cried.

"That's right. But the organs can't go to waste either. Lots of factors go into choosing the recipient. I shouldn't have to tell you this. We have to cross-match for maximum compatibility; therefore, more than one person might be prepped for surgery. Don't you remember when you were brought in for your transplant? All the tests we ran?"

"I had to wait a while," she said, but she knew she had very little recall from that frenetic time before her surgery.

"The transplant team had to make sure you were a good candidate medically. We wanted to be as sure as humanly possible *before* the surgery that the transplant would match. Because once you got the heart, there was no going back."

That stopped Katie cold and dampened her anger. He was right. Once Chelsea's heart was removed, it couldn't be put back if the new one didn't work out. "But Chelsea needs a new heart so much. And Jillian needs—" Her voice cracked. Josh took her hand.

Dr. Dawson nodded. "That's what I was trying to say earlier in the waiting room. We doctors have to weigh all the factors." He held out both his hands. "Do we save the one person who needs heart and lungs?" He elevated his palm as if he were holding a weight. "Or do we save three people—one who needs a heart and two who each need a lung?" He raised his other palm level with the first. "It's a tough call, Katie, especially when patients' needs are equal."

Numbly, Katie nodded. All the fight had gone out of her. She saw the medical dilemma with absolute clarity; a choice had to be made, and someone would lose. With the incoming organs, three people could be helped. Or all three organs could go to save only one. "What a terrible choice," she whispered.

"Actually, although the patients' needs may be equal, medically speaking, all factors aren't equal."

"What do you mean?"

"That's why we run so many tests. Medically, someone always has an edge. It's never equal medically. Tests help us separate and fine-tune our choices. Nothing's worse than giving a patient a transplant and then losing him. It's like we've lost two people at once—the recipient and the donor."

His gaze said, *"You're a survivor, Katie."* She was alive, and so was Aaron Martel. But then, Josh had told her that all along. Through her, he still had part of his brother living.

Dr. Dawson's beeper sounded. He switched it off. "I need to answer this."

She watched him swiftly disappear down the hall. "Maybe the donor organs are here," Katie told Josh without emotion.

"It's a little soon all the way from Columbus," Josh said.

She turned to Josh, tears welling in her eyes. "So, what do I wish for, Josh? Chelsea and Jillian are both my friends. I love both of them. Who do I want the doctors to save? How do I accept one friend's life over the other?"

The tears spilled down her cheeks. Josh took her in his arms, where she wept bitterly.

*   *   *

Ten minutes later, her mother came out of the ICU area. "Katie! I've been looking for you. Did you eat?"

Katie hurriedly brushed her damp cheeks. "I couldn't face the thought of food."

"Chelsea's regained consciousness. She's asking to see you."

Katie felt a rush. "Let's go."

Inside the glass cubicle, Katie took Chelsea's hand and squeezed. Her friend's eyes fluttered open and focused on Katie's face. "It feels like a truck ran over me," Chelsea mumbled. Her words sounded slurred, and Katie knew it was from pain medications.

"I got the license number. It won't get far."

Chelsea attempted a smile and groaned. "I didn't know I could hurt so bad." She turned her head so that she could see the heart monitor. "Funny how they put your heartbeat in a box. It's pooping out on me, isn't it? I'm afraid, Katie."

"Don't talk like that."

"Dr. Dawson told me there's a chance I may get a transplant today. Bye, bye, old heart. Hello, new."

"It's for the best. You'll see. You'll feel like a brand-new person."

"Dr. Dawson says there are others being considered. He didn't want me to get my hopes up . . . you know . . . just in case it doesn't work out."

"It *could* happen." Katie purposely avoided eye contact as she spoke.

"What aren't you telling me?" Chelsea asked suddenly.

Katie started. "I—I don't know what you mean."

Chelsea rolled her head on her pillow and made the line on the monitor screen jump. "Your face tells me you've got a secret."

"Not true! I don't know a thing."

"You know my hobby is observing people. And I know you're keeping something from me, Katie O'Roark." Chelsea tried to seize Katie's arm, but she was so weak, her hand dropped back to the bed helplessly. "Don't keep anything from me."

Shaken by the urgency in Chelsea's voice, Katie said, "I know others have been beeped."

"Others?"

"Others who need the organs." Katie squirmed. If Chelsea got the heart and Jillian died, Chelsea might never forgive Katie for keeping such a secret. Her voice shook as she managed the courage to mumble, "Jillian."

Chelsea squeezed her eyes shut. "I knew it. Deep down, I knew it. We have the same blood type. We're too much alike."

"Your intuition's too sharp for your own good." Katie felt tears edge her eyelashes.

Chelsea looked up at her pleadingly. "Never tell my parents this. Please don't ever, but go find her, Katie. Tell Jillian for me, I hope she's the one. Jillian deserves to be the one. Not me. Please, tell her, Katie. Please."

Sixteen

∽✦∽

I<small>T WAS EIGHT A.M.</small> before Katie could get into Jillian's room to talk to her. Josh waited for her outside in the hall. Lying in the hospital bed, Jillian seemed as frail as a baby sparrow to Katie. Her face was ashen, and dark circles under her eyes made Katie think of a war refugee. Jillian's mother was reluctant to leave her daughter's side, but Jillian begged to have some time alone with Katie. "Even ten minutes," she told her mother. Katie thought Mrs. Longado looked ready to drop.

When they were alone, Jillian reached for Katie's hand. "Daddy called from the jet half an hour ago. They were still in the air, but he said that he and DJ will be here soon. That'll help Mama."

Katie knew that the organs would be arriving soon too. And that meant making the final selection. A film of perspiration broke out on her fore-head. "Are you through with your tests?"

"I think so. How's Chelsea? Does she know I'm here?"

"I told her."

"I hate not being able to see her. We're right here in the same hospital, but we may as well be on separate planets."

"Well, that's what I'm for—Space Cadet O'Roark on call." Katie saluted and was rewarded by Jillian's smile, although the effort sent Jillian into a coughing spasm. When it was over, she lay on the bed gasping for breath. Alarm shot through Katie. "Should I ring for a nurse?"

"No. I want to talk to you while I can. I want you to tell Chelsea I'm pulling for her. She needs that heart."

A lump wedged in Katie's throat. "That's exactly the message she asked me to give to you."

"Just like her," Jillian drawled. "Always wanting me to go first."

Katie smiled. Even now, sick as she was, Jillian imparted humor. "Good thing Lacey's not in the competition. She'd insist she go first."

"If she doesn't shape up, she may be in the running for a pancreas transplant."

"You discovered that about her quickly. She hates having diabetes so much, she denies it. I don't know what we're going to do with that girl."

For a moment, neither of them spoke. Katie listened to the hiss of the oxygen tank. From outside the room came the name of a doctor being paged over the speaker system and the rattle of breakfast food trays being brought onto the floor. The trappings of the hospital never changed; the sounds had been the same when she'd been a patient.

"Thank you for taking me to Jenny House with you," Jillian said.

"It wouldn't have been right *not* to take you."

"And for including me on Amanda's mountain too."

"I know she would have approved."

"I wish I could see Chelsea," Jillian lamented. "You know what all this waiting makes me feel like?"

"I know what it made me feel like," Katie told her.

"But you weren't aware you were in some kind of competition for the heart you needed."

"That's true. What you're going through is worse."

"I'll bet this is what those Miss America contestants feel like while they're waiting for the judges to call their names."

"I don't think I get your meaning."

Jillian rotated her thin shoulders. "I've seen the girls on TV standing up on stage. They've been on preview for a million people. They've done their best, performed, looked their best. Then they just have to stand and wait for a computer to tally up a bunch of judges' scores and call out the winning name."

Katie was intrigued by Jillian's analogy. She'd never much thought about how awaiting a transplant could compare to a beauty pageant! But she did agree that waiting for a transplant donor *was* a little like a contest. "You may be right. I've watched beauty contests. It must be tough to stand there and keep smiling while you're waiting for your name to be called."

"And think about the expression on the winner's face when her name is announced."

"Stunned disbelief. I know that's what I'd feel."

"Maybe because no one expects it to be their name. You always think it's going to be the other girl's."

All at once, Katie got an inkling into what Jillian was trying to say. "You're *convinced* it's going to be someone else," Katie said slowly. "You *expect* it to be someone else. But down in your heart, you want to hear them call out your name."

"The announcer goes through the list of runners-up until he's down to two contestants. They stand there under the lights, wearing their hopes and dreams on their faces. They hang on to one another's hands. The announcer says, 'If for some reason the winner can't fulfill her duties as Miss America, then the first runner-up will be crowned in her place.'" Jillian paused to take deep breaths of fresh oxygen.

"Of course, no one wants to be second," she continued. "Everybody knows second-best never gets to wear the crown. But the announcer looks at his card anyway and says, 'First runner-up is . . .' Then the camera cuts to the winner's face, and the loser fades into the background. Because nobody ever remembers who *almost* won. Miss America is the important one. And that's the way it should be."

Katie considered Jillian's words carefully, feeling the girl's anguish. Jillian wanted to be a transplant recipient. She wanted to be the one chosen. But not at the expense of her best friend. "No matter how it turns out," Katie said to Jillian, "I believe something good can come out of the worst of situations."

"Like you and Josh?"

"Yes. That was a good thing that came out of a bad thing. Another was the One Last Wish Foundation coming out of Jenny Crawford's dying. And Jenny House coming from her grandmother."

Jillian sighed. "And if I hadn't been born sick, I'd never have met Chelsea. No matter how things turn out today, she was the best part of this whole thing."

"I'll tell her you said so." Katie knew their discussion had sapped Jillian's remaining strength. She said her goodbyes, promising to return once she'd checked on Chelsea.

Jillian's parents and brother came through the door. Katie hung back while they each hugged Jillian. She heard DJ say, "I brought you something." He dug in his jeans pocket and took out a piece of tissue.

"What is it?" Jillian wanted to know.

Katie couldn't help noticing that her brother's presence perked Jillian up substantially.

"Unwrap it and see."

The paper rustled. "It's hair from Windsong's mane, isn't it?"

DJ looked pleased with himself. "I curried him last night, braided the longest hairs together, and wrapped it up for you."

"You always know how to make me happy."

DJ looked pleased with himself. "I was planning on bringing it to you this weekend, but when Mom called this morning at the crack of dawn . . ." He didn't complete the sentence.

Again, Katie started toward the door. She stepped aside for two doctors entering the room. She felt her heart begin to hammer and knew something important was about to happen. Jillian's family instinctively gathered around her bed, like wagons circling a homestead for protection, and looked at the doctors expectantly. Katie was the outsider. She made herself leave so the doctors could talk freely.

She tossed Jillian a lingering look. Jillian's haunted eyes told her, *"I can handle whatever they say."* Katie stepped into the hall, where Josh still waited.

"What's up?" he asked.

"I think the decision's been made," Katie whispered. She felt lightheaded, as if she'd run too fast in a higher altitude. "Do you think they've come to say she's the one? Oh, Josh, if she is, then I have to get back to Chelsea."

"Hang on," Josh declared, grabbing her arm to keep her from bolting off down the hall.

Katie began to shiver as if a frigid wind had

blown down the corridor. "I'm scared, Josh. Really scared."

He wrapped her in his arms. "There's nothing you can do, Katie. Just like there was nothing I could do when they told me my brother was brain dead. Nothing except give away his body parts."

She realized that he was reliving the horror of his brother's death all over again. She felt awful, somehow responsible for making him go through it one more time because she'd asked him to come to the hospital in the first place. "I'm sorry," she said, through chattering teeth.

They clung to one another, but the holding didn't bring them closer together. Instead of a bond of sharing, she felt as if a blade of pain were dividing them. Separating and slicing them apart. Feeling shredded emotionally, Katie pulled away.

Josh's expression was one of devastation. Like someone who'd seen something too horrible to relate. *My fault*, Katie thought. All of it—from needing Aaron's heart to forcing Josh to be with her right now—was her fault. She might have turned and run away except that DJ came barreling out of his sister's room, almost knocking them over.

Katie seized his shirt. "What's wrong? What's happened?"

"The doctors said she has antibodies in her blood." DJ looked stricken, on the verge of exploding.

"I don't understand—"

"From transfusions during the surgery they did

on her a long time ago." Katie vaguely recalled hearing Jillian explain about an operation on her heart when she'd been a child. Surgery that hadn't worked. "She needs an extra test to check it out. The test will take another four or five hours." DJ's voice was shaking, and his fists were balled. "She won't be getting a transplant today. Not today."

Katie stood, stunned and rooted to the floor. Jillian Longado had just been named first runner-up in the contest for her life.

Seventeen

"Wait, DJ!" Katie called out, but DJ jerked away from her and took off down the hall. She spun toward Josh. "Please go after him. I have to go to Chelsea. I should be with her in case she goes into surgery."

"Go on. I'll hook up with you later."

She watched Josh head down the hall in the direction DJ had gone, then loped toward the elevators, grateful once again for Josh's presence. She shoved away the feelings of guilt and separateness she'd experienced minutes before. No time to sort things out now, she told herself. She stabbed the elevator button, but when a car didn't arrive, she went to the stairwell and jogged up six flights of stairs to the Cardiac ICU.

Once on the floor, she caught sight of a clock.

She'd known about the possibility of transplantation for hours—hours that had seemed to pass like minutes. Time was the critical factor. Surely, the organs had arrived by now.

Suddenly, she was struck by another thought. How many others had been paged? Dr. Dawson had said they could save three people if the decision was made to transplant the heart and both lungs separately. What if there was someone more critical or more compatible than Chelsea? What if Chelsea didn't get the heart either? Hadn't Dr. Dawson told her Chelsea was stabilized? That might mean more waiting for yet another donor.

Katie went to the ICU waiting room, but it was empty. She rang the buzzer in order to be admitted into the unit. A nurse answered through a speakerphone. "May I help you?"

"I want to know how Chelsea James is doing."

"She's been taken out of here."

Katie felt a wave of panic. "Where?"

"Ask the nurse at the main duty desk," the voice said from the small box.

Katie hurried to the nurses' station. A nurse looked up from a pile of paperwork, and Katie introduced herself. "Your family's been looking for you," the woman said.

"Where are they? And where's my friend, Chelsea James?"

"They've taken her down to the surgical floor. She's going to have a transplant."

Tears—part from relief, part from exhaustion—

welled in Katie's eyes. "All her tests checked out then?"

"Yes, according to the head surgeon. The helicopter arrived at the roof landing pad fifteen minutes ago. We've got three operating rooms going at once. Three recipients are being prepped for surgery. It's one of our biggest transplantation efforts to date." The nurse looked pleased.

Katie didn't wait for more discussion. She ran back to the stairwell and down the two flights of stairs to the surgical floor. In the surgical waiting room, which was made up of several small cubicles so that families could have absolute privacy, she found her parents and Chelsea's. "Katie." Her mother looked relieved when she came into the room. "Thank heaven you're here. They've just taken Chelsea in."

Katie's heart sank. She wouldn't be able to see her friend before the surgery. "I tried to get back sooner."

"She wanted to see you before she went under the anesthesia," Mrs. James said, twisting a wad of tissue in her hands. Her face looked anxious and full of dread. "She's so frightened. My little girl—"

"I told her you'd gone to visit with Jillian," Katie's mother said. "She'd seemed all right about it. She said Jillian needed you more now anyway. Any word on her transplant? Chelsea told us she was in line too."

"Mom, Jillian won't be getting a transplant. At least not at this time." Katie didn't add the information about the antibody test or that it was

Chelsea **who**'d bumped Jillian from her place on the list.

"I'm sorry. I know how her family feels."

Katie's dad patted the cushion between himself and Chelsea's father. "Sit down, honey. You look ready to fall over, and this surgery takes at least four hours."

Four hours! Katie didn't feel as if she could make it through four minutes in the small room. "I need to go find Josh and tell him what's going on. I'll be back soon."

She didn't wait for a response, but left the room quickly. Once in the corridor, she wasn't sure where to begin looking. She went down to the main lobby, which now bustled with visitors, medical personnel, and staff. Suddenly, exhaustion overcame her. She sagged against a wall and might have sunk to the floor if an arm hadn't slipped around her waist and held her upright. Startled, she turned and faced her benefactor.

"Garrison! What are you doing here?"

"There's a chapel down the hall," he said. "It's quiet, and we can talk."

She started to protest, but didn't have the energy. He led her to a room carpeted in blue and softly lit with pale yellow light. A Christmas tree stood just outside the doorway, and with a jolt, she realized that Christmas was coming. She'd lost her sense of time. Of seasons. Only the night before, she'd been at Garrison's party.

The chapel was empty, and she heard classical

music playing in the background. "Sit with me," Garrison urged.

She slid into a pew and bent forward, resting her forehead against the back of the pew in front and trying to regain her composure. He massaged the muscles in her neck. "Please, don't," she told him.

"Katie, talk to me."

She sat upright and twisted sideways on the cushioned bench until she was looking at him full in the face. "Why are you here?" she asked again.

"Looking for you."

"How did you know where to find me?"

"I've been calling your house since eight o'clock this morning. I drove over about nine-thirty, and your neighbor said he saw all of you leave in the middle of the night. I remembered your sick live-in friend and figured something must have gone wrong. I just decided to try finding you in the waiting room at the hospital."

"Chelsea had a heart attack. Once she was here, a possible donor became available. She was a match, and she's up in surgery now." Katie glanced around through bleary eyes, wondering what time it was. She couldn't seem to keep track of time this day. "I should get back."

"Not till we talk," Garrison told her.

"I'm all talked out," she replied with a sigh. "So much is going on. . . ." She had no history with Garrison the way she did with Josh, as Lacey had reminded her. Garrison didn't know about Jillian. He knew nothing about that part of her life. To

Garrison, she was an English project partner. A girl he'd invited to his party. A girl he'd kissed. She averted her eyes, remembering how she'd responded to his lips.

"I'm not going to go away, Katie. Not after last night."

She was tired, but not too tired to catch the deeper meaning of his words. He wasn't going to get out of her life simply because she couldn't cope with him in it. "Garrison, I honestly can't deal with you right now."

He smiled and tugged his fingers through her long, black hair. "I won't pressure you. I only want to remind you that once all this is over, you still have a life of your own."

"Do I?" For so long, her "life" had consisted of hospitals and sickness and dying friends.

"Aren't you going to run track in the spring?"

"I'm in training—"

"And how about a track scholarship to college? You told me you wanted one. Do you still?"

Katie shook her head to clear it. How long had it been since she'd thought about those dreams? She buried her face in her hands. "I don't know what I want, Garrison. I just don't know." Her sentence held a double meaning.

"No rush," he said, standing and pulling her to her feet. He held both her hands and looked down into her upturned face. For an unguarded moment, she felt naked and vulnerable. "When this is over," Garrison said, staring into her eyes, "and it *will* be over, I'll be in touch."

She didn't doubt him for a minute. "I love Josh," she said stubbornly.

He gave her one of his heart-melting smiles. "Loyalty is your strong suit, Katie. That's one of the things I like about you." He brushed the tips of her fingers with his mouth, sending a shiver up her spine. "Go check on your friend. I'll call you later."

She watched him walk out of the chapel, and once she was certain he was long gone, she left too. She was halfway to the elevators when she saw Josh. He stood by the gift shop doorway, watching her cross the lobby. Most certainly, he'd seen Garrison leave also.

"Chelsea's up on the surgical floor," she said as she came to him.

"I'll go up with you."

Katie braced for a fight, a barrage of questions about Garrison. Mercifully, none came. "How's DJ?" she asked.

"Mad. Mad at the doctors, the world, the universe. We talked, but I don't think I helped him much."

"Thanks for trying."

They stepped inside the elevator. The car was crowded, crammed with people on their way to visit sick friends and relatives. "How's Garrison?" Josh asked.

Katie stiffened. "Please—not now." Several people glanced curiously at her and Josh. She ignored them, shoved in more tightly so that her shoulder was pressed against Josh's. They stood that way, shoulder to shoulder, all the way up to the fourth floor, but they couldn't have been farther apart if they'd been standing on opposite ends of a gymnasium.

Eighteen

⌒⌒

THE FIRST SENSATION Chelsea experienced when she awoke for the second time was excruciating pain. In the recovery room, she had wanted to tell her doctor to let her die, that it hurt too much to wake up, but there had been a tube down her throat, and she couldn't speak. Now, at least, the tube was gone. But not the pain.

"Wake up, Chelsea." The voice called to her from somewhere above her head. "It's me—Katie. I only have five minutes, so wake up."

Chelsea forced her eyes open. When she could focus, all she saw was Katie's blue eyes above a green mask. Katie's hair was covered with a green paper cap, and she was wrapped in a green paper gown. "Your outfit's tacky," Chelsea managed to say. Her throat felt raw and scratchy, her voice sounded hoarse.

Katie's eyes crinkled, so Chelsea knew she was smiling. "You made it," Katie whispered. "You came through. You did even better than me."

Somehow, that notion pleased Chelsea immensely. "I feel awful."

"But you're *alive*."

"How long?"

"Until you wrinkle with old age."

Chelsea could vaguely recall her parents' faces. They must have visited her too. "I want out of here."

"They'll move you to your own room tomorrow. Then we can visit longer."

"I hurt so bad." Tears of pain pooled in the corners of Chelsea's eyes.

"I know. Have you seen your hands?" Chelsea felt Katie lift her hand off the bed and bring it closer to her face. "See," Katie said.

Chelsea worked hard to refocus. She saw her own fingertips in Katie's hand, the nailbeds bright and pink. "Did they paint them?"

Katie giggled beneath her mask. "No, silly. That's oxygenated blood pumped from your new heart all the way to the tips of your fingers. Your toes too."

With wonderment, Chelsea stared. She'd never seen her nails glow pink. Other sensations began to pour through her. The pain, yes, but a deep underlying feeling of coursing blood and a pumping heart. "I'm alive, Katie," she whispered.

"You sure are."

A cloud passed over her memory. "Jillian?"

"She's still in the hospital, and she sends her love. I'm the messenger. Got anything for her?"

"Tell her she's next. And it's worth it."

Katie's expressive eyes clouded momentarily. "She knows. She's waiting. Now, go back to sleep and heal quickly. So you can go tell her yourself."

Chelsea's eyelids slid closed, but the last thing she heard was the heart monitor beeping loud and strong and in perfect rhythm to the thumping of her perfect heart.

Chelsea continued to recover quickly. She tolerated the new heart amazingly well and adapted easily to the regime of antirejection medications. Dr. Dawson fairly crowed whenever he checked her over. She was transferred to her own room and was up walking three days after the surgery. Although in isolation, she was able to see her parents and Katie for longer periods at a time.

On the sixth day after the surgery, Lacey called. "Got time for an old friend?"

"Oh, Lacey! I feel so good. Sore and achy still, but wonderful anyway. I wish you were here."

"I'd love to see you too, but you know how it is —two days before Christmas, and what with my social calendar and all . . ."

"Don't do too much partying."

"There is no such thing."

Chelsea wanted to lecture Lacey about taking care of herself, but knew she'd ignore her. "So, I guess we're on for certain this summer with a return to Jenny House."

"I never doubted that you'd come through," Lacey said breezily.

"It was easier to go through the surgery than face your yelling at me," Chelsea joked.

"Smart choice."

"How's your home life?"

"No change." The line went silent, and for a minute, Chelsea wasn't positive Lacey was still on it. But her voice came through with a change of subject. "I sent your Christmas present to Katie's. You can open it when you go home."

"Gee, I completely missed out on shopping this year."

"Don't worry. I'll let you make it up to me. How's your rich little Texan friend?"

"I'm not sure. Not even Katie tells me much about her. I call her room, and we talk, but she's weak and can't talk for long."

"Well, tell her to hang in there from me."

Chelsea agreed, struggling to keep her composure. Every time she thought or talked about Jillian, she felt afraid. Chelsea thought that Jillian wasn't getting better, because if she were, people would talk about her more often. As it was, Chelsea had to pry information out of everyone. Her sixth sense told her that Jillian was extremely ill. She prayed that another donor would be found— and quickly.

On Christmas Day, the hospital dietitian saw to it that Chelsea got a turkey dinner with trimmings.

Chelsea ate with her parents in her room. They promised her a real Christmas once she was discharged. "I want to wait to open my presents when I get home to Katie's," Chelsea told them. "I don't want to do it here."

Late that afternoon, while her parents were out of the room, Chelsea received a visitor she'd never expected to see. The green garb was familiar, but the eyes over the mask belonged to DJ Longado. She felt her pulse race and realized that, old heart or new, he had the same effect on it.

"Hi," she said, wishing she looked better. There was still a tube coming out of her chest, and she couldn't remember the last time her hair had been washed. "Merry Christmas."

"Merry Christmas," he returned. "I hope you don't mind my visiting. Jillian asked me to."

Chelsea knew it was foolish to feel let down, but she did. If only he'd come because he wanted to. "How she's doing today?"

"Not any better."

The news scared Chelsea, mostly because DJ sounded so low. "Did you have Christmas with her?"

"We put a tree in her room. Mom and Dad had all our ornaments shipped from back home. The tree looked good, but it sure didn't much feel like Christmas."

"I wish I could go visit with her."

"She says to tell you the same thing."

An awkward silence fell, and Chelsea searched her brain for something to say. But all she had to talk about was her operation, and that was nothing to discuss with DJ. "So, how's your girlfriend, Shelby?"

"She's being a pain."

His candor took Chelsea by surprise. "How so?"

"Can you believe she pitched a fit because I wasn't going to be with her over Christmas? I mean, my sister's trapped in a lousy hospital a thousand miles from home, and all Shelby talks about is not having me around to take her to a few parties." His eyes blazed above his mask. "I just don't understand her. How can she act so selfish?"

Chelsea was certain that if Jillian had heard his question, she would have had a snappy answer about Shelby's lack of character, but there was nothing Chelsea could say. And after the hateful way Shelby had treated Jillian, there was nothing she *wanted* to say.

"Sorry," DJ said. "I didn't mean to dump my silly problems on you."

"No problem."

"You hurting?"

He looked curious, and Chelsea felt more like a medical freak than a fifteen-year-old girl trying to achieve normalcy. "Yes, I hurt," she told him. "I have lots of physical therapy ahead of me, and that hurts too."

He nodded, but seemed distant, if not slightly hostile. She didn't know why, but hoped it wasn't her fault. He edged around the foot of her bed. "Isn't this you and Katie?" He picked up Chelsea's photo taken that summer at Jenny House.

"Yes, along with a couple of friends. The girl in the middle died."

He set the framed photo back down with a disgruntled mumble. "That where you took Jillian over Thanksgiving?"

"Yes. To Jenny House. We had a good time together."

He gazed off at the far wall. "Well, she sure isn't having much fun now."

His words sounded almost like an accusation. Chelsea wondered if there was any way she could talk Dr. Dawson into letting her pay Jillian a visit. "Please tell her to remember her promise about coming back to Jenny House this summer."

DJ stared at her with a look so piercing, it unnerved her. "She wanted me to give you this." He changed the subject, dug into his pocket, and brought out a wad of tissue.

She took the tissue and carefully unwrapped it. Inside lay a pair of garnet dice. "Aren't these from Jillian's Monopoly game?"

"She wants you to have the game for a Christmas present."

Chelsea gaped at DJ. "But I can't take her one-of-a-kind Monopoly set."

"Yes, you can." DJ sounded defiant. "If that's what my sister wants, then that's what she's going to get."

Chelsea was dumbstruck by his angry voice. And hurt. "I—I didn't mean to sound ungrateful."

"It's not your fault." He backed away, his voice contrite. "I need to get back to her room."

"Tell her thank you, and that I'll call her later today."

"I'll tell her."

He was almost out the door when Chelsea blurted, "I really did want her to get the transplant, DJ. I wanted it to be her instead of me."

He turned slowly and gave her a long, lingering look. "But it wasn't her. The doctors decided she had to wait for another donor, and that's what we're doing."

"One will come along. Tell her not to give up hope."

"It isn't hope she lacks," DJ said quietly. "It's time."

Once he was gone, Chelsea began to cry. More than anything, she wanted to see Jillian and hear her laugh and joke again. She wanted her to have the same chance at living that she'd been given. Why was life so unfair?

Chelsea swallowed against the fist-size lump in her throat, picked up the wadded white tissue, and sat staring at the blood red dice, wishing there was something she could do.

Nineteen

"IS THERE ANYTHING I can do to help you, Katie?"

Josh's question brought Katie out of her mental stupor and back into the library, where they were studying for exams. "My mind wandered off again, didn't it?" she said apologetically. "I can't seem to concentrate on anything."

"Do you want me to take you home?"

"It's worse there. Every time I walk past Chelsea's room, I think about poor Jillian."

"Think about Chelsea instead. Three weeks since her surgery, and she's doing great."

She knew Josh was trying to be helpful, and she appreciated it. "Did I tell you that when I saw her today, she had persuaded Dr. Dawson to allow her to go visit Jillian?"

Josh looked surprised. "I didn't think they'd let her out of isolation."

"She'll come out sooner or later anyway, and she's really improving. They'll take her down in a wheelchair, and of course, she'll have to wear a mask, but the trip will be good for her. She's going crazy not being able to see Jillian."

"When will they let Chelsea come home?"

"Another three weeks if she doesn't have any rejection setbacks."

"Rejection." Josh shuddered. "I remember yours."

"Well, it can happen." Katie didn't want to think about herself. She only wanted Chelsea to be all right and the transplant center to find Jillian a donor.

"Come on," Josh said, taking Katie's hand. "Let's stretch our legs."

She figured she might as well; she certainly wasn't getting any real studying done.

The library lobby was crowded for a Tuesday night. Outside the glass doors, the January wind whipped snow across the parking lot. Katie watched it swirl in the light of the lampposts, and identified with the fine white flakes. It was how she felt on the inside—powerless, tossed and blown by the cold winds of life.

The automatic door slid open, and Garrison walked in. His head was down, his hair wind-whipped. When he looked up, he was staring straight into Katie's eyes. She glanced away, as she felt Josh stiffen beside her. She hoped Garrison would ignore her, but he didn't. He came over and said hello to her and Josh.

"Any change in your friend?" he asked.

"Nothing new," Katie said. She saw him every day in class, but although she was polite, she kept him at arm's length. Their paper had earned an A-plus and the teacher's handwritten comment, "Brilliant! Well done." She was glad for that. Her A in honors English had been the bright spot in the weeks following a return to classes.

"So, I'll see you tomorrow," Garrison said.

When he'd gone, she glanced at Josh. He wore a scowl. "It's not a crime to talk to him, you know," she said.

"Did I say anything?"

"You don't have to." Katie wasn't angry. She simply didn't have the energy for it. She kept busy. She ran every morning at the YMCA track. The high school season began in March, and she was determined to be ready for it. She attended classes. She studied. She saved Saturday nights and Sunday afternoons to be with Josh. She was trying, really trying to hold their relationship together. Ignoring Garrison wasn't easy, but she did it.

"Maybe we'd do better if we studied someplace else," Josh said. His look was challenging.

She bit back words about how juvenile he was acting and that it was a big library and they could certainly share it with Garrison. "Fine by me," she said.

"Wait here. I'll get our books."

"Maybe it would be better to go to my house,"

she said. "That way, if Chelsea wants to talk to me, I'll be there."

Josh agreed and went for their books, and together they walked outside into the biting cold night.

"They've put Jillian on a machine, Katie." Chelsea's voice quivered as she spoke. They were in the elevator, on their way to Jillian's room in an ICU on another floor of the hospital. A nurse stood behind Chelsea's wheelchair, looking sympathetic, but saying nothing.

"What kind of a machine?" Katie asked.

"An extracorporeal membrane oxygenator." Chelsea pronounced the words distinctly because she'd been practicing them. "ECMO for short. It's an artificial heart and lung. It's doing the work of her heart."

"Doesn't sound good to me."

Chelsea struggled to keep her emotions under tight control. Dr. Dawson had warned her that Jillian had been placed on the machine and that she'd been heavily sedated. He'd told Chelsea that Jillian would be unable to respond to her visit. But Chelsea was convinced that showing up in Jillian's room, that talking to her friend, touching her, would somehow make a difference.

Staff watched as Chelsea and her entourage came down the hall. The hospital personnel seemed so pleased to see her recuperation progress. "You give us hope. Makes us remember why we do our jobs," one of the nurses had told her.

At the doorway of Jillian's room in the ICU, Chelsea almost lost her nerve to go inside. She felt the clutch of fear, her lifelong companion. Katie reached down and took her gloved hand.

Jillian was on the bed, lead wires from monitors snaking to her chest. Two tubes protruded from her groin area, from the femoral arteries, and led to the ECMO machine. One tube carried her oxygen-poor blood into the machine, where it was oxygenated by a special membrane, and the other tube carried the blood into her body to her oxygen-starved system. The machine was eerily quiet, adding to the life-and-death role it was playing in Jillian's life.

Jillian's family hovered near her bed, the strain of their vigil showing on their faces. Chelsea's eyes immediately sought out DJ. His eyes were red-rimmed, and his hands were clutched in tight fists. Slowly, DJ and his parents stood as Chelsea was wheeled into the room. Mrs. Longado came over to greet her. "Your doctor asked if you could come."

"I *had* to see her," Chelsea said. "Thank you for letting me."

DJ walked to join his mother and placed his arm around her shoulder. "My sister's dying," he said. "The machine can't keep her going for more than a couple of days." His gaze automatically went to the front of Chelsea's bathrobe, to the spot where her new heart beat strongly within her chest. If there had been a way for Chelsea to reach in, pull it out and offer it to Jillian, she would have.

"Hush," his mother said. "No use talking like that."

"Maybe a donor will come in," Chelsea told him.

"Not likely," DJ replied, stepping aside.

The nurse rolled Chelsea closer to the bed. Jillian's pale, gaunt face reminded her of a picture of a death mask, stark and white and chillingly hollow-looking. Jillian's face resembled the mask so strikingly that Chelsea flinched. "Can I touch her?" she asked.

"Yes."

"She can't feel anything," DJ said.

Chelsea reached for Jillian's hand anyway. "Hey, Jillian. It's me, Chelsea. I came to . . . to let you know . . . I miss you." Chelsea was forced to pause because of a thick clog of tears wedged in her throat. "Katie's here too. We want to remind you how much you mean to us, now and forever."

The beep of monitors and the hum of machinery were the only sounds in the room.

"We should return to your room," the nurse said gently.

Panic seized Chelsea. "I don't want to go back yet." She knew instinctively that this would be the last time she saw Jillian alive, and she couldn't leave her, didn't want to leave her.

"Please, Chelsea—" the nurse said.

"You can't make me leave." Of course, it was an

idle retort. She was still weak and didn't even have the strength to pull herself out of the wheelchair.

Katie crouched down and took Chelsea's hand once more. "Listen to her. Don't put yourself in harm's way."

Chelsea allowed herself one long, lingering look at Jillian and began to cry. The nurse pulled the wheelchair backward, and Katie walked next to it, her hand resting on Chelsea's shoulder.

"Thank you for coming," Jillian's mother whispered. "Thank you for caring."

Mr. Longado echoed her words. DJ said nothing.

Once she was safely in her room, Chelsea lost her composure and sobbed uncontrollably. Katie hugged her. Chelsea looked up through her tears and said, "This new heart they gave me is breaking, Katie. It's breaking in half."

The following day, late in the afternoon, when Katie came into Chelsea's room, Chelsea didn't have to hear the words—she saw from Katie's face that Jillian was gone. "When?" Chelsea asked.

"About half an hour ago. They told me her heart just gave out. Her family was with her."

"What happens now?" Chelsea asked.

"They're flying her back to Texas."

"Everybody goes home one way or the other, don't they? Amanda went home too."

Katie stood close to the bed, tears brimming in her eyes. " 'She died too young,' " she whispered. "That was something Mr. Holloway said to me about Jenny Crawford," she explained. "We were standing in the lobby at Jenny House last summer, looking at her portrait together, and his voice was full of pain and love. He said, 'She died too young.' I think he loved her when they were both young. I think he still loves the memory of Jenny Crawford."

Chelsea nodded. "Too bad love can't hold off death."

"I've always thought love was stronger than death," Katie said.

Chelsea turned her face toward the wall and said nothing more.

Katie picked up the phone and dialed Lacey's number in Miami.

Twenty

❧

"CHELSEA, I'M CONCERNED about you." Dr. Dawson stood at the foot of Chelsea's bed, wearing his most serious expression. "If you don't start eating, if you don't start improving mentally, I won't be able to release you. Don't you want to get out of here?"

Chelsea all but ignored him. She didn't care. She simply didn't care.

"Some depression is normal after transplantation, but this isn't. I want you to talk to Dr. Cummings."

Dr. Cummings was the head shrink. She and Jillian had been part of her therapy group when they entered the transplant program together. "I don't want to talk to anybody," Chelsea said. "Please go away."

"You've been given an extraordinary opportunity," Dr. Dawson continued. "And you're doing so well tolerating your new heart. Don't give up now."

A cold sweat broke out on Chelsea's forehead. Fear seized her, and for a moment, she couldn't catch her breath. Her heart pounded, and she was certain it would beat itself to death. "I hate this crummy heart," she told him. "I feel exactly the way I did before—with my old heart. There's no difference. I'm going to die, and this heart will have gone to waste. You should have given it to somebody else. Somebody who would have taken better care of it."

Dr. Dawson studied her thoughtfully. "It isn't good for you to feel this way, Chelsea. It won't contribute to your healing process. You're alive and well, and I want to see you stay that way. Dr. Cummings will be in to talk to you tomorrow."

She continued to ignore Dr. Dawson, but when he left, she felt alone and desolate. *What's wrong with me?* She couldn't answer her own question. Why were all the old fears, the old symptoms of fear, paralyzing her, keeping her from working with her doctor, her physical therapist. Not even Katie could cheer her up.

A nurse breezed into the room. Trailing behind her was a man carrying a VCR. "This came for you today," the nurse said, waving a videotape. "The letter accompanying it said it was to be shown to you immediately. Dr. Dawson's okayed it, so let's set this up for you."

"Where'd it come from?"

"The post office," the nurse said with a smile. In a matter of minutes, the VCR was hooked to the TV in her room, and the tape had been inserted. The nurse brought over the remote control.

When she was alone, Chelsea sighed. She didn't want to watch some stupid tape. Why couldn't everyone just leave her alone? After she'd stared at the blank screen for a time, curiosity began to get the best of her. With resignation, she pushed the Play button.

"Hey and howdy." Jillian's face sprang onto the screen.

Chelsea gasped and dropped the remote control. She fumbled around on the bed for it as Jillian's voice came clearly into the room. "I was going to write you a letter, but you know we like to do things BIG in Texas. Besides, I've always wanted to film myself. Dramatic, huh?" She mugged for the camera.

Fascinated, Chelsea continued to watch. Jillian was sitting up in her bed at the penthouse, telling Chelsea that she had taped the message weeks before. Sunlight was coming from one side, lighting up Jillian's hair, turning it to copper fire.

"So, you're probably asking yourself why I am doing this instead of talking to you in person. Good question. It's because I feel pretty good today. Also, I've got lots to say. Besides, you're a captive audience, and you can't talk back!"

She grinned, and Chelsea found herself smiling in return at the TV screen.

"This is really for your eyes only, Chelsea James. You can show it to Katie and Lacey if you want, but I've got some things to say, mostly just for you." Jillian's bright smile faded. "On the serious side: I'm tired of sitting around and waiting for this transplant. But I'm also scared it won't happen for me. If it happens for you, and it doesn't happen for me, then I need to let you know some things. Plus leave you some instructions."

Chelsea swallowed hard. It was weird watching and hearing Jillian. More real than any VR game she'd ever played. *She's dead*, logic reminded her. This is only an image.

"You know you're my best friend ever. Too bad we met the way we did, too bad we need the same thing from medical science. But if you get a transplant and I don't, then I expect you to do something with your life. Grow old, for starts."

Again the quick smile.

"But mostly, I want you to keep in touch with DJ. Now, I know what you're thinking. I'm taking advantage because I know you like him. Well, I'm not. I'd ask you even if you didn't think he was the neatest thing since sliced bread." She leaned forward. "I'll never understand how he got the blond hair and good looks and I got red hair, freckles, *and* a bad heart and lungs. Go figure."

Chelsea found herself smiling again.

"You're probably thinking, 'So why does a prince like DJ need looking after?' For starters, he's not going to take to my dying and leaving him behind. He acts tough, but underneath, he's a marshmallow. I can't go off and leave him alone with Shelby. Nope, can't let that happen.

"Also, Mama and Daddy have each other to look after. But DJ . . . well, he's only got me, and I may not make it."

Chelsea felt a shiver. How uncannily accurate Jillian had been about her future.

"So, where does that leave *you*, Chelsea James? I hope it leaves you smiling and happy. I hope it leaves you with a brand-new heart and a whole new outlook on life." On-screen, Jillian stared directly at the camera, held up her finger, and shook it as if Chelsea's nose were in front of her. "I mean this! Forget your virtual reality games. Go after the *real* thing.

"Don't worry about me. I'll be up in heaven, remember?" She pointed her finger upward. "And when I get there, I'm going to look up Amanda and Jenny Crawford, and see if we can't think up some mischief together."

Her bright smile flashed, then faded. She leaned forward, as if imparting a secret. "I never figured I'd get old, Chelsea. But I would like to have gone falling off a cliff or being bucked off a horse. If you get a transplant, you have to do everything for both of us. It's your sacred duty. And don't forget, I'll be up there"—she pointed again—"watching you."

Chelsea pushed the Pause button on the remote control when it was obvious that Jillian was through talking. The picture of Jillian's face froze on the screen. It was blurry, as photos stopped in motion are, but it was her—red hair, freckles, smile, and all.

Slowly, Chelsea climbed out of bed and shuffled over to the TV set. She stood in front of the screen, staring long at the image of her friend. Her fingers touched the cool glass, and she traced the lines of Jillian's face. *"Live,"* her friend had said.

Chelsea placed her hand on her own chest. Her fingers felt the thumping rhythm of her heart—a gift from a stranger. The beat said, *Life*. It was hers. A second chance. She knew she shouldn't blow it. For Jillian's sake. For her own.

Chelsea rewound the tape and removed it from the VCR. She glanced at a clock and saw that her session with her physical therapist would soon begin. She still had a long way to go to be as healthy and active as Katie. She felt a surge of resolve. *Yes, a lot of work to do.*

She was grateful and ready to live. And she was no longer afraid.

RL 4, IL age 10 and up

ISBN 0-553-28008-2

Published simultaneously in the United States and Canada

*Bantam Books are published by Bantam Books, a division of Bantam
Doubleday Dell Publishing Group, Inc. Its trademark, consisting of the
words "Bantam Books" and the portrayal of a rooster, is Registered
in U.S. Patent and Trademark Office and in other countries. Marca
Registrada. Bantam Books, 1540 Broadway, New York, New York
10036.*